Juliette Akinyi Ochieng

Carmel Coast Publishing Enterprises (2010)

Tale of the Tigers

Published by Carmel Coast Publishing Enterprises

Cover Design by Carmel Coast Publishing
Enterprises – Graphics Division

Printed in the United States of America

ISBN 978-1-61623-206-1

A special thank-you to my mother, my step-father and my great-aunt for always believing in me.

Many thanks to my editor Caren T. Handley for knowing what I mean without me having to tell her.

And thanks to my friend, C. Lamar Powell, CEO of Carmel Coast Publishing Enterprises, for helping me to fulfill a dream.

To Robert

all the best

Juliette

For Rob Smith

Brown Penny

I whispered, 'I am too young,'
And then, 'I am old enough';
Wherefore I threw a penny
To find out if I might love.
'Go and love, go and love, young man,
If the lady be young and fair.'
Ah, penny, brown penny, brown penny,
I am looped in the loops of her hair.

O love is the crooked thing,
There is nobody wise enough
To find out all that is in it,
For he would be thinking of love
Till the stars had run away
And the shadows eaten the moon.
Ah, penny, brown penny, brown penny,
One cannot begin it too soon.

--William Butler Yeats

Where do I find it?
It hides itself well
Yet 'tis my doom
To be under its spell

Prologue

She had to pay. There was no getting around it. She had to pay for stepping in where she didn't belong--to pay for inserting herself in Tau business, in man-business, in the Black Man's business, and it would be so easy to do. They wouldn't even have to touch a hair on that nappy head of hers or do anything to that fine ass, and that ass was fine; he knew from close up. As a matter of fact, he was getting excited just thinking about it. Maybe, he should call her...

No point in it. Besides, she had a new man; for now, that is. Daniel seemed like a straight-up brother. They would be doing him a favor.

Trevor laughed as he picked up the phone to send out the call to his minions, his fraternity brothers. And after that, they would make Felice LeCroix pay for her insolence.

Tale of the Tigers

<u>Chapter One</u>

It wasn't the world that nineteen-year-old Felice LeCroix thought it was--the one that she had been told it was. And now, she was paying for that fantasy: her life was in ruins. Her grades were scraping the floor and her reputation preceded her on the campus of New Mexico University. *Blame it on this place. You've always hated it.*

Without consulting her, Felice's parents had decided to move their moderately successful restaurant business to

Albuquerque from Los Angeles right after she had graduated from high school. She was a California girl, born and raised, used to being close to an ocean and used to having the delights of a large city at her fingertips. New Mexico seemed to be a brown, barren, land-locked wasteland in comparison. "Land of Enchantment?" To Felice, "Land of Boredom" seemed like a more accurate motto for the state and its largest city. There was nothing like Venice Beach or the Universal City Walk here. There was no Melrose Avenue, nor a Hollywood Boulevard, where she and her girlfriends would innocently walk down the street on Saturdays at high noon and gawk at the freaks. The only two malls here closed at six o'clock on Saturdays in this tiny, boring desert town. Additionally, there were hardly any black people in the entire state.

She had asked her parents if she could stay in L.A. with her grandma Anna, but they had refused, citing her frequent disobedience.

"Your grandmother is retired and in her sixties," Felice's mother had told her. "She has raised her own children, and she should not have to put up with you. You are *our* responsibility." Having been only sixteen when she had graduated from high school, she had to do what her parents said. She knew some girls who would have defied their parents under such conditions, but she wasn't up to that particular task. A little minor defiance, maybe, but she knew how far to push her luck.

So, she had moved with them and what a fiasco it had turned out to be. But, the voice of reason spoke to her. *Mom and Dad didn't do this,* she thought. *You have nobody to blame for this mess but yourself.*

She got up and threw herself onto her bed. How had things gotten to be so bad? She could continue to fantasize—this time about the mess magically disappearing, but she knew that as soon as she set foot on campus at the beginning of the new semester, the pointing and sniping would begin anew—and that she deserved it.

Shit.

During high school, Felice had been an indifferent student, showing only occasional signs of interest in history and math classes. Having barely graduated with her class, the only reason she had been accepted to a four-year university like NMU was because of her high College Board scores; NMU had offered her a full academic scholarship. She had been barely seventeen years old at the beginning of her freshman year, having skipped one grade in elementary school. Fearing the worst after her dismal high school performance, her parents had been relieved and overjoyed at her acceptance to NMU.

"Maybe, you can finally show a little initiative," Vetra LeCroix had told her. "I know you were bored in high school, but NMU is a demanding school. I know you'll do well. Just put forth some real effort."

"Okay, Mom," Felice answered obediently in the time-honored way she had of answering her parents. Whether she'd do what they asked was another matter, however. "Could you please try to talk Daddy into letting me stay in the dorm?"

"Now, you know there's no way he's going to agree to that, and he's right."

"But if I had gone to Spelman, I would have had to do that anyway."

"Somehow, I don't think that your father was going to let you go back east to school at any rate," Vetra LeCroix had sighed. "Even, if it was Spelman. You haven't shown us yet that you can be trusted."

It was again time for the patented answer. "Okay."

Felice chafed under her parents' strictness; she had been seventeen, not thirteen. She should at least be allowed to go to one of the campus parties that often occurred on weekends during a given semester. But Joseph LeCroix would have none of it.

"I went to that school. I know what goes on at those parties and that was twenty-five years ago! I don't want to even imagine what your 'friends' do for entertainment in 1991! The answer is no."

"Dad, come on. I can't just go to school, come home, study, and sit up under you and Mom all the time. I got to have *some* fun."

Joseph thought for a minute. "Fine, I tell you what. You can go to the party and I will come and pick you up at eleven thirty. Okay?"

That was the end of that particular round of negotiations. There would be no party going for her, probably not until she was thirty. Felice was not about to endure the humiliation of having her imposing father pick her up from a party at eleven thirty, especially when she knew that they generally lasted until about three. So, during her freshman year of college, her life had consisted of going to school, coming home, and even on occasion, studying.

Now, it seemed that her attempt to liven up her life had blown up in her face. She was the campus pariah.

What had she been thinking? Answer: she hadn't. She knew that now. Or if she had been, it had been wishful thinking. She thought that she lived in the "modern" age, where a woman could do what she liked and with whom she liked. Liberation...what a joke that word was.

She could track the course of her slide into disrepute so clearly, in hindsight. Adrienne Anderson, her only remaining friend, had warned her.

In the summer session after her freshman year, Felice had begun to do volunteer clerical work at the African American Cultural Center on campus. Though the racial make-up of NMU's student enrollment reflected Albuquerque's population, only 4 percent of NMU's students were black. And when one walked into the center, one would understandably think that one were at a historically black university. It was the hub of all activity, specifically involving black students and the base of the campus' African American Student Union.

Working for the A.C.C. was a great way to meet people—or so Felice had thought. However, she had made only two friends--Adrienne, and a girl named Vonetta Hall. Being in a place where there was a constant influx of activity, Felice figured that friendship would come to her, though that had not been her prior experience. Solitude had been her constant companion growing up. But, now it was time to fully grow up and out of her self-imposed shell—or so she thought. Others seemed to make friends as naturally as breathing and so could Felice, if she simply put her mind to it. However, when she had expressed her interest in becoming more active in black community activities, Adrienne had warned her to be cautious.

"Get involved, but don't let any of them into your actual life," she had advised.

"What?"

"Don't get too involved with them and don't let them know your business."

Adrienne, a varsity basketball player, was an active participant in many of the activities involving the African American Student Union. However, she was not a member of the union, nor was she a member of one of the two traditionally black sororities that had chapters at NMU.

"Groups can be useful," she had told Felice. "But they also have the tendency to breed assholes. Take the 'Greeks' for example. They survive on divisiveness and problems, which is not surprising, considering their background."

Before Felice had gone to college, she had known nothing of fraternities and sororities. Her interest was peaked. "What's the deal with them anyway?"

"You know about the Greeks, right? I mean the real ones. Ever heard of the book, *Stolen Legacy*, by George G.M. James?"

"No."

"That's not surprising, since it was published in the fifties. My mom bought it for me when I was about twelve. It seems that the ancient Greeks stole most of their culture from the ancient Egyptians, according to George James."

"So what?"

"Felice, the Egyptians were 'black.'"

"Wait a minute. No they're not. They're Arabs. I've seen a lot of them on TV." Then Felice remembered something she had thought upon first seeing the late Egyptian president Anwar Sadat. He had looked just like her Uncle Richard.

Adrienne looked at her friend with impatience. "The media puts out the ideas that it wants us to have. I've *been* there, Felice. I've seen the ruins. Those people were mostly black people. Funny how TV always manages to focus on the white-looking ruins whenever they're filming in Egypt.

Oh yeah, and sure most of the Egyptians are Arab *now*, but we're talking about thousands of years ago. Is the racial make-up of *this* continent the same as it was a thousand years ago, or even three hundred years ago?"

"Okay, you have a point. So, what does this have to do with the black Greeks?"

Adrienne sighed. "The very basis of their existence is deception, girl. Black Greeks-what an oxymoron!"

"It's pronounced 'oximeryn,' with the accent on the second syllable."

"Whatever. I think my pronunciation applies better. You get the point anyway, right?"

"I guess. But how do you steal somebody else's culture? Do you snatch it out of their pocket and run?"

Adrienne looked at Felice as if she had sprouted a second head.

Felice grinned and decided to let it go. She thought Adrienne might be a little paranoid about groups, and she saw no harm in associating with the black people who were "Greeks." How wrong she had been. Did these "Greeks" have the older Greeks to blame for their behavior? And she really didn't care about all of that "history" anyway. All she knew now was that she was paying the price, for not having listened to Adrienne about the here and the now in the first place.

As always, the shower felt good after practice. Kevin Hart opened his eyes and looked down at the drain as soap, sweat, dirt—and a little blood--washed away. Saturday's game would be a tough one, against UCLA, number one in the Pacific Athletic Conference and number three in the nation. His own school was number one in its conference, but number fifteen in the nation. During its thirty-year history, the Western Athletic Conference had rarely had a football team in the top twenty.

The practice had been a good one. His passing average had dropped a bit in his senior year, but he was still the number five-rated quarterback in the NCAA. He felt the now-familiar nervousness he usually felt before a big game. Not nervousness per se, but of the standard anticipation-caution emotional mix. At six feet five inches, he was a large enough man to withstand most of the hits that came with the quarterback position. However, he had a tendency towards slimness, so, unlike many of his positional counterparts, he had a strenuous workout regimen that had bulked him up to a powerful two hundred thirty pounds, from the wispy one hundred seventy that he had weighed as a freshman.

So, Kevin could take a pounding with the best of them. This quality, along with his height, speed, and accurate passing arm, made him a formidable and feared presence on the football field. It also made him a big target. Defenders made it a point to try to take him down, sometimes viciously. During his junior year, he had suffered a late-season fracture of his right leg, after one such hit. NMU had still been conference champion that year, but his injury had effectively ended his school's hopes for a national championship.

So, unlike most young men, Kevin had a healthy sense of his own vulnerability. *I'll be careful,* he thought as he towel-dried his brown, straight hair. *But we'll still beat the Bruins down!*

I hope.

As they stepped out of the entrance to NMU's practice facility, Kevin and Malik Hayes, Kevin's main receiver and best friend, had an immediate entourage. The two had met three years ago, upon Malik's first road game as an NMU Tiger, after he had become Kevin's road roommate. Room assignments had been given alphabetically, by last name.

After that game, the two had instantly become inseparable. However, the friendship was not without its bumps. Kevin, who had grown up in Albuquerque, had not had much contact with an inner-city. Conversely, the Detroit-born Malik, in spite of his intrinsic good nature, came with all the preconceptions and defenses that young men required for survival in an inner-city. Additionally, Kevin was white and Malik was black, which could have created its own minefields. At the beginning of their relationship, it nearly did.

Like all college athletes, Kevin and Malik were big fish in a small pond. However, they were more than the average "big men on campus." Due to their exceptional abilities, they were nationally known, a separate breed even from the average athlete. Consequently, they received special perks and privileges nearly everywhere they went, not only on campus, but all over town: free meals, free cab rides, free everything, if they wanted it. However, Kevin had been taught by his father that the word "free" usually came with some kind of price, even if the price wasn't money. As a result, his father provided him with a generous allowance. So, often, Kevin would refuse the constant gratis goods and services that he and Malik were offered, and would insist on paying both of their tabs. Malik didn't like it at first.

"What? You think you gotta hand out crumbs to the poor black boy from the ghetto? My daddy may not be some crooked lawyer, but he makes an honest living."

Kevin didn't understand. "What's your problem? When I pay for a meal for a poor *white* boy from Chicago, like Strazinski, he doesn't say shit but 'thank you.'"

"Oh, so now I'm supposed to be grateful for crumbs from the Massa's table?"

"Wait! So buying dinner for somebody is a racial issue now? I need to take notes. Got notes for the test?"

Malik paused. "So, you told me you don't have any brothers and sisters, right?"

"Right."

"Well, I do. I had an older brother. He's dead now. I have another older brother, who basically should be dead. He's a crack-head. I have an older sister who's in the Army. She's, like, the star of the family. For the moment, that is. But I am the entire hope of my family. You? You do what's expected of you. Your father, your grandfather, and your great-grandfather before him graduated from NMU. I am going to be the first person in my family to graduate from college. I was one of the very damn few to graduate from high school. My father gave me something called pride."

"Hey, my father gave me pride, too."

"But, it's something special when it comes from a black family, especially families like mine, where only half the children grow up to be something called respectable. My sister is respectable. My father has always told me that I should be respectable. So, that's what I'm trying to be. One of the things that my father taught me was that to gain respect, you never take anything from anybody. Go and get it for yourself. That's why I feel strange when I take your charity, especially with you being white."

Kevin thought for a moment. "It's not charity and it has nothing to do with respect. I know a little bit about the experience of black people in this country, but I never really sat down and thought too long about it--never cared to do it. We're just teammates; friends. But, now that I think about it, when we started running around together, some of the white guys on the team--and you know who they are--acted like I was making a pact with the devil.

"I understand about pride. I don't quite understand where you're coming from as far as the black and white thing, but I understand about pride. As you pointed out, my dad told me that graduating from this university was a matter of pride. So I guess I get it, but listen to this, deal with this: I'm not doing this because I think you're a 'poor black boy' that needs my help, you know..."

"Watch that boy shit."

"Hey, you're the one who called yourself that! Can I finish?"

"Please do, oh Great White Father."

Kevin sighed. "In the words of your buddy, Conway, 'stop trippin'." He went on. "This is just what friendship is to me. If I have a friend and I have something, my friend has it too. That's all there is to it. It has nothing to do with charity or anything like that. I know my dad has money and he gives it to me. So if you're my friend, I'm going to give to you. I don't give a damn what you look like or how much money your dad has. That's all there is to it. It's got nothing to do with pity or anything like that. So, like, can I just do this?"

Malik looked at him. 'Yeah, you can, because I'm broke as hell." They both laughed, breaking up the tension.

"I got an idea," said Kevin. "When we get to the NFL and you're getting paid millions of dollars to let guys like

Deion Sanders chase your ass around, you can pay for *everything.* How about that?"

"Deal." They had shaken on it.

Now, as the two surveyed the scene before them, they glanced at each other with some dismay. On one side of the "entourage," there were the heavily made-up and perfectly coifed white girls, mostly blond, Kevin's groupies. On the other, there were the mostly braided and weaved black girls, along with a smattering of Latinas and white girls, Malik's groupies. The two men glanced at each other after a quick survey of each bunch.

"We don't have time for this," Malik said to the women impatiently. "We've got a big game tomorrow. Don't y'all have classes or something?"

"Come on ladies, don't go away mad," said Kevin more gently. "You know we're gonna beat those pretty boys from L.A. Malik and I just need to get our game plan down pat. We'll be looking for you at the game." He smiled. The women moved away, wearing puzzled and disappointed expressions, and let the two men pass.

"Good snow job," said Malik later on. "But, why do you care what those hos think, anyway?" They were now strolling along NMU's tree-strewn campus. The mid-

December sun glared on their shoulders, providing uncharacteristic heat, considering the season.

"One of those 'hos' is helping me with my economics class. It would seem kinda ungrateful to tell her, 'get outta here, bitch, I'm busy.'" They both laughed.

Later, as they walked and talked on the campus, they were each constantly gawked at or greeted by name, mostly by people they didn't know. Nearly everyone on campus knew who *they* were, however.

As they traded friendly insults, Kevin noticed one young woman pass them, barely giving either of them a glance.

"Hey, you know that girl?"

"Who?"

Kevin turned around and pointed at her. "*That* one."

Malik turned to see the shapely, retreating backside of a tall, slender, dark brown-skinned woman, striding purposefully away from them. After a moment's thought, he decided that he recognized that backside.

"That's Felice. She works in the African American Cultural Center sometimes. She's a sophomore. Heard she's got a little hoochie in her."

"Damn, not another one for you."

"Not me, man. But, some of the brothers from the Taus gave me the tip on that one. Several of them been there. What? You thinking of crossing the line?"

"Not if she's just like the rest of 'em."

They walked in silence for a bit. Then Kevin turned to Malik.

"Have you ever noticed that the 'hoochie patrol' is a little one-sided? How come you get the rainbow coalition, but I get only the white ones?"

"I don't know. Let's ask 'em."

"I don't want to talk to any of 'em, more than I have to. I want to know what *you* think."

"Ain't we supposed to be going over the game plan?" Malik said with a smirk.

"Forget the game plan. That's all we've heard about since August. I want to talk about something important: women."

"Fine. Let the Bruins sack your ass."

"Be serious." Kevin smiled. "What else do you know about uh...Felice?"

"So you *are* thinking about crossing the line!"

"What is the big deal? You got all the women--black, white, and indifferent. You and the rest of the 'brothas,' cross the line all the time!"

"And you get just the white ones, and the skank ones at that. Are we going to the 'black man, white man' thing again now?" Malik asked knowingly.

"No...hell, I don't know."

"'Cause if we are, I gotta put on the 'brotha' hat."

"Oh *great*. The 'brotha' hat."

"Yeah, the 'brotha' hat." Malik mimed putting on a hat. "Now, I'm speaking from the 'brotha's' perspective."

"Did you learn the word 'perspective' in your freshman English class?"

"Fuck you, white man. I learned to say that in English 101, too."

"Right. I *know* you didn't learn it by actually doing it."

Malik flipped him off.

"Yeah, you said that already. Sorry, I'm not thinking about crossing *that* line."

"Anyway, this is the 'brotha's' perspective: we can take your women at will, as compensation for you taking ours."

"Me?"

"Your ancestors. Why do you think that black people have such variation in skin color?"

"I don't know. I never thought about it."

"The reason is this: during slavery and for a hundred years afterward, it wasn't a crime to take advantage of a black woman. A white man could get some black stuff whenever he pleased. Married or single, 'eight to eighty, blind, crippled, crazy.' Where do you think that expression came from?"

"Damn, you have been paying attention in English class!"

"Don't try to play it off, white man! Now, after the Civil Rights Movement and Affirmative Action and all that shit, we feel that we now have a right to your women."

"'My' women?"

"Yes, your women. 'Brotha' hat off. So, what do you think about that?"

"I don't know. Sounds kind of stupid to me and not quite right. From what I've seen, the white girls chase after you all, for the most part, not the other way around."

"Some of them do, some of them don't. Your little friend, Mandy, always looks at me like my skin's gonna rub off on her if she gets too close."

"Yeah, well, she just doesn't know what a charming personality you have," he smirked. "And besides, Mandy's okay, just too big a mouth occasionally."

"She's in one of my seminars. Every time I say something, she looks at me like she expects me to break out in a jigaboo dance or something.

Kevin rolled his eyes. "Damn, you're paranoid! Everybody's not looking to burn a cross on your lawn. Mandy probably just wishes you'd shut the fuck up sometimes. Back to the subject: how come the black girls don't chase after us?"

"I don't know for sure. I guess you'd have to talk to a black woman to find out," Malik said slyly.

"Yeah, well maybe I will, later. Right now, I've got to head to the library and hit some books. The dorm is probably noisy as hell right now."

"Like always. I gotta late class to go to. Later." The two men parted.

<u>Chapter Two</u>

One month into the beginning of the spring semester
of 1992, Felice sat alone in one of the semi-circle shaped,
high-backed seats in the lounge of the Quad, NMU's student
cafeteria. She was reviewing her World Literature assignment
with a slight sense of deja vu. In addition to the dread she
felt at having to show her face on campus, she had to repeat
three of the classes she had failed the previous semester.
She had only one new class--American Government.

After the fall of her reputation, Felice had considered
opting out of college altogether. She could join the military,
something she had thought about upon graduating from

high school. But back then, she had been too young to join on her own, and her parents had adamantly refused to sign the parental consent form that seventeen-year-olds were required to have to join up. Now, however, she was eighteen and could do what she liked. *Boy, would that tick Mom and Daddy off, she* had thought, with perverse amusement. She could enlist and be gone before her parents even finished having their shit fit.

Or, instead, she could go back, defiantly, with her head held high. She couldn't do anything about her reputation, but she could show that she was more than just a pretty face, a nice body, or a piece. Despite her mediocre grades in high school and here in college, she knew that if she would just put forth a modicum of effort, if she simply went to class regularly, she could get a least all Bs. If she actually studied, she might get an A or two. Her mother and father had been telling her this for years. So what if she didn't have a social life? Hadn't it always been that way? The only difference in this case was the reason behind it.

Intensive study was best done at home or in the library. However, Felice had found that the lounge area of the Quad, the campus cafeteria and meeting place, was a good place to do a cursory review of notes, or a quick cram right before a test. Usually, it was nearly as quiet as the library here, with only the distant murmur of the main cafeteria drifting over. It was also a good place to hide. Felice might hold her head high, but she wouldn't look for trouble.

Suddenly, her concentration was broken by high-pitched female laughter. She looked up to see a group of about six, heading towards the seat across from her. There were five girls and one tall guy, the last of which she immediately recognized. Who in Albuquerque didn't recognize him? His face and name had been splashed all over the sports pages and the news for years now. She immediately turned her attention back to her task, mentally turning their chatter down to a drone.

Her reading assignment for World Lit was *Divine Comedy* and she was right in the middle of the "Inferno." *Comedy is right,* she thought. It was hilarious in a ghoulish, Stephen King sort of way, demons farting and such. Who knew that a thirteenth-century dead white guy had such a gross sense of humor? She might have, had she gone to class last semester.

Enough already! Stop beating yourself up. She was enjoying the story, but she was already forming a rebuttal to it in her mind. Her ideas about a supreme being were vague. Though she referred to God as "He" whenever she thought about "Him," she was more likely to believe God was an "It." It was benevolent and loving (except when somebody made It mad), and was greatly concerned with justice, but what was its nature or its name? Christians, Muslims, and Jews all purported to know, but who really knew except those who had already left to join It? Felice certainly didn't.

However, she had much more defined ideas of what hell might be like. In the "Inferno," hell was a generic place with standard, set punishments. You went to one part of it if you were an adulterer, another if you were a murderer, still another if you were a blasphemer, and so on. In the story, there was even a man who "seemed to hold all of Hell in disdain," as Dante had put it.

She decided that God was probably a lot smarter than this Dante guy. Heaven might be generally pleasant and ambiguously lovely, but hell would surely be much more personalized. God, being omnipotent and all, would simply have to know the subconscious horror of each individual person that It had created. Surely, It would get together with Satan and say, "Hey, Stupid! Here's the info on *this* one."

Armed with such intimate information, she could see Satan greeting the unrepentant sinner at the gates of hell.

Is your idea of hell being in an enclosed space? We got that. Is extreme hunger or extreme thirst your idea of hell? Is it being in a room with your mother-in-law? We got that. We got all of that and ever so much more. We got a quadrillion of 'em.

Her reverie was broken by an odd feeling. The droning had stopped and she looked up to see that tall guy was looking directly at her. The girl sitting on his left started to say something to him, but he shushed her.

"Hi," he said to Felice.

"Hi," she answered uncertainly, unsure as to whether he was speaking to her or not. The withering looks that the group of girls gave her, however, cleared up any doubt. It was as if eyes could cause combustion. She tried to turn back to the "Inferno," but it seemed as though it was much hotter in the real world. She quickly stuffed her belongings into her backpack, put her coat on and left.

But as soon as she stepped out of the Quad, she immediately stepped into her own personal, self-fashioned Hell. She nearly collided with Andre Carter, one of the Tau fraternity brothers. He wasn't one of the ones she had slept with, but they all knew what had happened and had spread their knowledge of it in their revenge against her.

"Hi, hoochie," he leered at her. "When we gonna get it together?"

"Asshole," she muttered, just loud enough for him to hear as she hurried away from him. He turned and tried to catch up with her.

"Oh, so I'm an asshole now," he said loudly. "You're the one who slept with half my frats. I just want to know when you gonna' hook the other half up!"

His progress was halted by a powerful hand on his shoulder.

"Leave her alone, Mr. Carter," said the voice belonging to that hand. Andre whirled around and looked up into a pair of hazel eyes that he didn't particularly want to see. Adrienne Anderson, six-feet tall with golden-brown dreadlocks, captain of the women's basketball team and Felice's best friend, looked down at him. She was a beautiful woman, whose physical strength wasn't immediately obvious. However, when she grabbed Andre's shoulder, he had no choice but to stop.

"Don't you have a class to go to or something?" she asked him, meaningfully.

"As a matter of fact, I don't!"

Adrienne had to slightly bend down to put her nose about a centimeter from his. "Well, I'm sure that you wouldn't like your frat brothers to find out that you got your ass kicked by a woman, so *be gone*." He backed up ever so slowly, so as not to appear to be running, but Adrienne could sense his fear, as well as see it in his eyes.

"Get outta here, boy," she growled. He turned and sauntered away.

"My heroine."

Adrienne sucked her teeth. "Girl, you've been reading too much of that World Lit nonsense."

The two began walking toward the mass of academic buildings. Adrienne was one of the few women Felice knew who was taller than she was.

"Nice pick, O great Amazon Basketball Woman."

"Just returning the favor. Do the Taus only allow fools to pledge?"

"It looks that way, doesn't it? But ole 'Dre didn't waste any time gettin' gone when you stepped in, so he's not *that* stupid. Forget him. Something strange just happened to me in the Quad."

"Another chapter in 'These are the Days of Felice's Life?'"

Felice grinned complacently. "Pretty much. You know Kevin Hart?"

"Quarterback of the football team."

"Right. I was sitting in the lounge, looking over my World Lit stuff and I felt somebody looking at me. So I looked up, and across from me, was Kevin and a bunch of white girls. He was staring right at me. One of the girls started to say something to him, but he told her to shut up."

"Really?!"

"Then, he just goes, 'hi' to me and I say 'hi' back. Then, I got the hell out of there 'cause them girls looked like they were going to have a lynching with me as the guest of honor."

"I'll bet they did," Adrienne giggled.

"It was weird. I had seen him looking at me before, but I wasn't interested in some big, goofy white boy. I don't care if he is the quarterback of the football team. But, he is kinda cute. So tall! Not that I'm that wild about big guys, but he's good looking'...for a white guy. Good looking, period."

Adrienne was appalled. "Felice, you're *not* going to do that, are you?"

"Why not?" asked Felice innocently.

"What do you mean why not? He's *white.*"

"Well, I never really looked that hard at white guys. Some of them are cute, but I never really thought about them like that before."

"He's *white*, Felice. You know what white people are."

"Excuse me, but uh...isn't your mother white?"

"You know she is, but that's beside the point."

"How is it beside the point? Part of you is white."

"Well, that's not my doing."

"You have a good relationship with your mother, right?"

"Yeah, but Mom is different."

"How in the world is she different?" asked Felice skeptically. "She's still white."

"But, Mom understands things. Hey, she married a black man back in the seventies. When my father left, she could have given me up for adoption or had an abortion, like so many white women did who got pregnant with black babies. But she didn't. She's also the same white woman that took her half-black child to Africa and gave her books to read like *Seize the Time,* and *Wretched of the Earth,* and *The Isis Papers.*

"So, what's the difference between your mom and, say, somebody like Kevin?"

"Oh, y'all are getting married now?"

"Don't play 'dumb jock' with me," said Felice with exasperation. "You know what I mean. What is the difference?"

They stopped and sat on one of the benches that were strewn around the campus.

"He's a man," Adrienne answered. "White men have been running this country, and running *over* black people and Indians, and every-damn-body else in the world for hundreds of years."

"Well, it seems to me that these white men were given birth to and nurtured by white *women.*"

"Yeah, but they run their own women over, too."

"Excuse me, but many of these white women are the ones that have enjoyed the fruits of the white man's conquests. Anyway, what does any of this have to do with the right-here and the right-now?"

"Now who's playin' dumb? You know exactly what it has to do with the right-here and the right-now. One of the white man's most frequent conquests is that of the black woman. Look at how light your dad is. You remember you told me how he got that way?"

"Yes, my great-grandmother was raped and so were thousands of other black women, and that's the reason many of us--except for folks like you--have such light skin." Felice recited this last like a litany. "This still doesn't have anything to do with *this* subject. It's a different day. Anyway, all the guy did was say 'hello' to me. He hasn't asked me out or even talked to me."

"Yeah, but from what you described, the guy is interested." Adrienne flashed an evil grin. "Boy, wouldn't there be some crap then! You and the Big White Man on Campus, doin' the 'jungle fever' thing. The Taus would have a flippin' fit, like the hypocrites they are!

"Why should they care what *I* do? They don't care about me. My biggest mistake was even talking to them, much less having anything to with them."

"Yeah, I know," said Adrienne uncomfortably.

"I know it's hard for you to talk with me about this. What I did was...disgusting. But, I did what I did and I can't change it. I was stupid and I didn't understand what was going on, though I should have. It's my fault for not thinking."

"Well, I can't sit here and judge you. You found out the hard way what they were like."

"No pun intended."

Adrienne grinned. "It's good that you can laugh about it."

Felice shrugged. "It's either that or jump off the top of the Quad, something I'm not considering--at this point, anyway."

"You know I've been talking about the Greeks and their crap ever since my freshman year. You took your fall because you were defending *me*."

"Yeah, but I gave them the ammo to get back at me. And thanks for not saying 'I told you so.'

Felice paused, and then continued. "They're like a pack of wild dogs. Five of them were going to *beat up* on one person, and a woman at that!"

"They're smart, like a pack of dogs, too. They all know that if it had just been one, I'da cracked his head open!"

"They're supposed to be so 'pro-black.' Yet, they do things like gang up on one black woman, cut another black woman's reputation to shreds, and cheat on exams? They're the biggest hypocrites on campus."

"Well, I *did* dime on one of their frats about the test and you did threaten them with the police for ganging up on me.

"I also slept with three of them...best friends. There. I said it."

"Well, they screwed up your life way more than mine."

Felice sighed. "My relationship with Daniel pretty much went down the tubes after that."

Adrienne looked at her curiously. "You never told me what exactly happened between the two of you."

Suddenly Felice's watch beeped. She looked down at it.

"It's ten-thirty! My World Lit class is almost over. I swore to myself that I wouldn't miss any more class. Damn, damn, damn!"

"Sorry, girl. I know you're on probation. I didn't mean to make you late."

"Hey, it's not your fault. Anyway, I might as well stay here and tell you now. So here's the story: I went to Daniel's room like I used to do everyday at my lunch hour. When I knocked on the door, he opened it just wide enough so that I was only able to see him and not the room. All he was wearing was a pair of shorts. Since I'm a little taller than he is, I just looked over his shoulder. There was a girl in there; short, blond hair. She was in his bed with the covers over her. All I could see was her head and her bare shoulders. Shit, she wasn't even cute."

"'It ain't the cutey, it's the booty.'"

"Guess not."

"'It ain't the hoochie, it's the koochie.'"

"Okay, okay, enough!" Felice laughed in spite of herself. "Are you trying to make me feel better or worse?"

"Sorry. So ole Danny-boy has a little jungle fever, too..."

"It was more than just that. He set that scene up on purpose; he *knew* I came by at that time. I found out from him later that Trevor and some of his little flunkies had spilled the beans to him about me. That was Daniel's way of breaking it off," Felice said sadly. "Pretty cold, but how can I blame him? I'm a hoochie."

"You're not a hoochie." Adrienne said gently. "You exhibited a little hoochie behavior, but you're not one. You made mistakes. Sure, all these punks around here are going to call you one, but what the hell do they know?"

"I know. Anyway, when I talked to Daniel a couple of days later, he asked me if it was true. What could I tell him but 'yes'? I tried to tell him that it had nothing to do with us, but he just couldn't deal with it. Over Christmas break, I considered leaving school, just saying 'forget it' and going in the military or something."

"But you came back. That shows courage; just like the courage you showed when you saved my behind. Called 'em every kind of Uncle Tom in the book. No wonder they had to get back at you."

"Now, *I'm* the one that's considered the scum. How's that for 'BS'? Nobody, besides you, will speak to me now, none of the black people, anyway."

"Like I said-dumb." Adrienne's evil grin was back. "They'll start speaking to you when you start dating Mr. Kevin 'I'm-the-big-Kahuna' Hart."

"Yeah, but I bet you that I will not like what they have to say." They laughed.

"Fuck 'em," said Adrienne with defiance, pushing her lion-colored mane out of her face. "Do what makes you happy."

"Hold up! A minute ago you were telling me that I was consorting with the enemy."

"Yeah, well maybe you are. But, it seems to me, that too many black people are our own worst enemy."

* * *

Two weeks later, Felice was in Crown Mall not having a good time. She was one of the few women in the world who absolutely hated shopping. She especially hated buying gifts, because, if she didn't have a specific gift in mind, she was forced to 'shop'--that is, walk around to three or four stores in order to decide what to buy. There were a few other things she found more boring, but not many.

On top of that, there was no one that she dreaded buying gifts for more than her father. Upon receiving a gift, he had the habit of saying something like, "Oh, that's such a nice gift. Thank you, sweetheart," and then never using the gift. The man was absolutely impossible. However, his birthday was at the beginning of March, so she had to get something soon. Once, while in a store with both of her parents, she had seen him eyeing a leather jacket with some interest, but such a thing was a bit out of her price range- about a thousand dollars out of it, to be exact.

In Dillard's department store, she walked by the cologne department...boring cologne. Joseph hardly ever wore any cologne except for when he and his wife were going out, and since they had opened the restaurant, that was next to never. Felice had noticed that her father still had the same bottles of cologne that he had bought before they moved to New Mexico.

If only I had more money, she thought with frustration. *Just like everyone else wishes.* She didn't hunger too much for riches. She only wanted a nice house, nice furniture, a nice car, a few nice clothes, and enough left over to be able to give to those that she loved, like her father. Sure, he was a pain sometimes, but he was hilarious and pretty cool, too. She'd at least like to be able to get him a stupid leather jacket. She couldn't remember her parents ever taking a vacation and going anywhere. She'd like to send them both to the Caribbean or Africa or Europe and out of her hair for a while. They both need a rest and so did she.

As things were, however, her father spent up to eighteen hours a day in the restaurant. Her mother usually would come home early to bring Felice's little brother home from school, but neither of them had very much time for their children, or each other. Felice had to admit that they had far less time to hassle her anymore. Her father would arrive home around ten, stinking from sweating his way through dozens of orders of Creole recipes. He'd then take his shower and go straight to bed, barely having spoken to his wife or his two children. His son would already be in bed. Felice promised herself that one day, both her parents would be able to relax and that she would be able to give them anything they wanted, and even things that they didn't know they wanted yet.

Maybe one day-but not this one. Felice walked by the shirts and ties. *Cologne, shirts, and ties...oh my.* She wanted to get something that she knew he would treasure and use, something that he was interested in, something that was relevant to *him,* not just anybody.

If that was the case, the first thing she needed to do was get out of Dillard's and probably get out of the mall, period.

She walked out of the department store and looked around. Right in front of the department store's exit was a bookstore. That was the ticket! Her father was a voracious reader, though he rarely had a lot of time for it anymore. However, reading was one of the few things for which he made extra time.

She walked in. In the Black/African American interest section, there were slim pickings. There wasn't much demand for such things here and Dad already had a good-sized selection of such books anyway. However, the Latino and Native American interest sections were large and eclectic. Her father liked history. Maybe he would like to read something about Native Americans, a subject that he had only a superficial knowledge of, as far as Felice knew. One title, *In the Spirit of Crazy Horse*, jumped out at her. She picked up the thick, heavy book, opened it and read the jacket. It was about an FBI raid against the American Indian Movement, the injustices that followed and the history behind it. Kind of like what happened with the Black Panthers. Her father would be enthralled. She tucked the book under her arm.

Intent on what she was doing, she nearly walked into someone. A very tall someone, she quickly judged, since, being rather tall herself, she found herself looking at the second button on a man's lumberjack shirt.

"Oh, I'm so sorry. I wasn't looking where I was going," she said amiably as she looked up. It was Kevin Hart.

"Hi," said a smiling Kevin.

Felice felt an unexpected surge of happiness. Why? She fought it down. "I didn't mean to run in to you. I was so intent on getting this book that my mind was a world away."

"That's okay. I get that way sometimes, too. Hey, don't you go to NMU?" asked Kevin casually enough.

"Yes."

"I've seen you around campus a few times."

"I remember you saying 'hi' a couple of times," she said, feigning nonchalance. "You're the quarterback of the football team, aren't you?"

"Yeah, I am," he sighed.

"Well, you don't sound too happy about it," she chuckled.

"It's not that I don't like it. Obviously, I love it or I wouldn't be doing it. It's just that sometimes I'd just like to be anonymous, you know? I just like to be alone, I mean really alone. Like, I like to come here to the bookstore. Nobody expects a jock to know how to read, much less want to *buy* a book."

Felice laughed. "Yeah, you got a point there." She looked at him. His gaze was almost tangible. He wasn't exactly undressing her with his eyes, but seemed to be trying to look into her--the actual her. Being undressed by men's eyes was something she was starting to get used to, but this intense scrutiny, was something else again.

The gaze only lasted a few seconds. He seemed to shake himself out of it.

"What's your name?" He asked, as if he didn't already know.

"Felice."

"Felice...Felice...what?"

"Felice LeCroix."

"LeCroix. French, eh?"

"Yes. My dad's people are Louisiana Creoles."

"Really? That's interesting. My name is Kevin Hart."

"Yes, I know." They laughed and shook hands.

"Well, you might not have. I didn't want to seem too conceited." They smiled at each other.

"Did you grow up here?" he asked.

"Actually I grew up in L.A-Los Angeles, that is, not Louisiana. But my dad grew up here. My grandparents moved here from Louisiana before my dad was born."

"Interesting. Ever been to Louisiana?"

"Yes, I have," Felice frowned, loathing the memory. "It was hot and muggy and they have mosquitoes the size of airplanes. I hated it."

"That probably made for some pretty big bites."

For whatever reason, the mosquitoes had loved her. She had black marks on her legs for six months after that trip to her 'homeland.' "You wouldn't believe how big."

"Yes, I would. I have some relatives who live in south Texas. In case you're interested, my German great-grandparents migrated from back east and we've been in the southwest ever since. My great-grandfather was one of the first graduates from that illustrious institution that we call, uh...home. So, do you like it here? It has to be real different from L.A."

"It bites the big Kahuna."

Kevin threw back his head laughing. "I'll take that as a 'no.'"

"That's right. There's next to nothing to do here. Everything shuts down here at sunset. Even this mall shuts down at six today, on a Saturday, no less. Not that I like shopping, but six? Be serious. Saturday is when everybody has time to shop late. Talk about hick town."

"Careful, there," Kevin said mildly. "You're talking about my home town."

Felice recognized the taste that suddenly was present in her mouth: the taste of foot. "I'm sorry, I didn't mean to insult..."

Kevin grinned. "Don't worry. It *is* a hick town. I should know."

"It's just that I didn't want to move here, but I was sixteen when we moved, so I had no choice."

"How did you like high school here?"

"I had already graduated when we moved."

Kevin whistled. "Wow, pretty impressive." Then he paused and looked at her a bit nervously. "So...how old are you now?"

"Eighteen."

"Oh. So are you buying a book for a class?"

"No, it's a gift for my dad. It's his birthday on the first of March."

"No kidding? I'm here looking for a gift for my dad, too! It's his birthday, on the first of March!"

"Wow! My dad will be forty-five. How about yours?"

Kevin grinned. "The same age. Maybe they're twins, separated at birth."

"I don't know. Does your father try to control your every move?"

"Not too much. But maybe it's because I'm not a girl. Face it. A woman brings out the worst in a man, especially, if the woman is his daughter. I'm an only child, but my cousins catch it from my uncle, so I know what you're talking about."

"What kind of book do you want to get for your dad?"

"I don't have a clue. My dad's a lawyer, so he has books all over the place. I was beginning to think that buying him a book might be kind of boring. What kind did you get? That might give me an idea."

She showed him the book. He opened it and quickly read the jacket.

"A good idea, but my dad already has a lot of books on Native American culture. He's done some work for the tribes."

"Does he have any other interests?"

"He likes golf, but I don't think he'd want to read a book about it."

Felice thought for a second. "I have an idea. If you'd like, I'll show you a place that might have something he'd like."

"Okay," Kevin said casually. "Maybe, between us, we can figure out what an old guy might want."

* * *

After Felice paid for the book, they walked out of the store, with Kevin feeling both a sense of rightness and a sense of fear. As they walked, they continued to make casual, "getting-to-know-you" conversation. He could smell a light scent of coconut whenever he got within a foot of her. He covertly glanced down at Felice's short hair. That's where the scent was coming from. He resisted the urge to plunge his nose into it. She was so...naturally beautiful, no makeup--no fake nails. And she didn't wear what Malik referred to as 'ho' clothes, though she had the body for it.

But, hadn't Malik said she was a 'hoochie?' Kevin found that he didn't care. Besides, she didn't seem to have the standard prerequisite: an air head. A girl that brought her father a book on the American Indian Movement couldn't be *too* stupid. She talked about her family and her friends, not herself, also not airhead-standard. She was asking him a question.

"Kevin..."

"Huh? Oh, sorry. What did you say?"

"I asked if your father liked western wear."

"Yes, actually, though he's probably the only man in New Mexico that doesn't own a cowboy hat. Wait! That's it. Lair of the Outlaws is on East Central. How about it? Want to come help me pick one out?"

* * *

Later, after they had found a present for Kevin's father, they were riding in his restored sixty seven convertible Volkswagen Bug, having left Felice's car (actually her mom's car) at the mall.

"He's going to love this thing," Kevin said, reaching back to pat the large hat box. "It's about time he got something to protect that bald head of his from the sun."

"He doesn't have a comb-over, does he?"

Kevin laughed. "No. He used to, but I convinced him he could catch more babes without it."

Felice paused. "What happened to your mom?" she asked gently.

"She died when I was ten," said Kevin, matter-of-factly. "A drunk driver plowed into her car at an intersection and pushed her into on-coming traffic."

She was appalled. "I'm sorry for you."

"Thanks. Since then, it's been just me and pops. He's had a couple of dates in the last few years, but nothing earth-shaking. He says there's not much to choose from."

"He doesn't like the little young girls?" Felice thought of how many times she had been hit on by men older than her father.

"No, surprisingly enough. I thought all those old geezers liked the young stuff. I even told him to go get one. But, he said that he didn't like them. Too stupid."

"Well, hooray for your dad."

"My mom was a historian, with PhDs coming out of her ears, so I guess he's spoiled."

Kevin felt good. He hadn't talked about his mother to anyone in the years since her death, not even--especially not even--to his father. Somehow, however, it seemed fitting to talk to this woman about the only woman in his life that had meant something to him.

"Gosh, I'm starved," he said. "Hey, let's go get some lunch...just to thank you for this idea."

Felice started to say no, however, her ever-insistent stomach spoke for her. "Where?"

"How about Mexican?"

That was the end of any of Felice's hesitation. "Let's go."

He watched her eat, with some admiration. Kevin was used to dating women who ate like birds, ever concerned about the extra calorie or two. It got on his nerves. This one, however, ate like a defensive lineman, and wasn't shy about it. Felice had ordered one of the large combo plates and was putting it away. She was so slender; he wondered where she put it.

"So, what team are you going to next year?"

"Uh...I'm sorry. What did you say?"

"Which team for you? Next year, I mean. You graduate this year, don't you?"

"I'd like to go to the Niners, but so does everyone. I'll probably get drafted high though and go to some loser team, like the Rams." Kevin flashed her a lop-sided grin.

Felice made a face. "Yuck! The Lambs. Nobody in L.A. likes them. They've stunk since Rosenbloom died. I've hated them since they moved out of the Coliseum, which is right in the heart of South Central L.A. Too ghetto, I guess. Maybe you could go to Green Bay. I predict that they will be the up and coming team in the next few years. Smart receivers. Perfect for you."

Kevin looked at her with wide eyes.

"Don't look so shocked," Felice laughed, pleased that she had obviously impressed him. "I used to hate football just like almost every other female."

"What changed your mind?"

"I realized that I couldn't hate something that I didn't know anything about. Actually, my dad made me realize that. At the beginning of one season when I was about thirteen, he challenged me to sit with him every Sunday and watch the games with him, while he explained the rules to me. He was a cornerback in college. By that end of the season, I had become a fan forever."

"Your dad sounds like a pretty cool guy. What school did he go to?"

"NMU, but only for two years. He dropped out and went into the Army. After he got out, he finished up at Cal State L.A."

"I wonder if he and my dad knew each other. What's his first name?"

"Joseph."

"I'll ask my dad about him. So, Miss Football Expert, did you check us out last season?"

"I don't like college ball that much. The personnel changes too often. But, to answer your question, yes."

"So, what's your critique of my year? Don't hold back. Be honest." Kevin braced himself.

Felice grinned at him playfully. "Your average has dropped some, but you're still good..."

"Thank you."

"However..."

"Uh-oh. Here it comes."

"You rely on your size and speed too much and you pass to Hayes too much as well, though it's understandable. He outclasses the rest of your passing options."

"Are you sure that Coach Reynolds didn't do a body trade with you? You sound just like him."

"I'm sorry." Felice was a little embarrassed. "I'm being a little arrogant, telling you how to run your business."

"Hey, I asked. Besides, it's kind of nice to talk to a woman for a change about what I love and have her love it, too."

Felice took a sip from her third glass of lemonade.

"So, what do *you* love?"

Felice thought for a second. "I just recently found out that I love school. Well not school, exactly, but learning new things. I've got a class this term. In it, I've found out all sorts of things that I didn't know about the American system of government."

"Yikes! Now, you sound like my father."

"I take it you're not into school that much."

"Not enough hours in the day. Wait. That's not the truth. I get C's and the occasional B. I guess I could do better if I put in more effort. A couple of my teammates manage to play well and be good students. Like Malik. Did you know that he was on the Academic All-American list this year?"

"No, I didn't. Wow, pretty nice. He's probably one of the few that's on that list and the regular All-American list as well."

"And, the only African American male athlete to have both honors for ten years. Did you know he's graduating this year? He was a year behind me. He's probably a genius. I think he puts on that comedian/horndog exterior just because that's what most people expect him to be."

"Sounds like you two are pretty close."

"He's my best friend. You know him?"

"Of course I know *of* him, like I know of you. I've seen him around the B.S.U. African Cultural Center a couple of times. I used to work there."

"Well, now you *know* me."

"A little bit I guess...what time is it?" She glanced at her watch. "Four o'clock? How long have we been here?"

"I'd say about four hours." Felice looked around the small restaurant. When they had first arrived, it had been full. Now, the two of them were the only customers left. It had emptied out and she hadn't even noticed.

"We gotta go!"

"Okay. Let me pay and we're outta here."

Fifteen minutes later, in the mall parking lot, they stood outside her car. The door was open.

"Thanks for the lunch," she said smiling. "My mom told me not to get into cars with strangers, so I guess I should thank you for not being a serial killer too."

"You're welcome, on both counts."

They looked at each other wordlessly for an instant.

"Well, I guess I'll see you at school." Before Kevin could reply, Felice quickly jumped into her car. Without looking at him, she drove away.

Chapter Three

"Hey, Mom, company's here."

"Adrienne, what did I tell you about that?"

Adrienne turned to Felice with a grimace as Felice stepped through the doorway of the Anderson household.

"We've got company," she tried again, hoping that her mother would tone herself down. As usual, it didn't work.

"I don't care. I told you to call me Laura months ago."

Felice grinned at Adrienne's exasperation. Adrienne's mother was definitely different, just as Adrienne had warned her. Felice looked around the living room of her friend's Santa Fe house. African, Native American, and Asian art had made a grand, international union here. But, somehow everything seemed to fit.

"It's the art U.N. in here." Adrienne commented, reading Felice's mind.

"Hi, I'm Laura Anderson. You don't straighten your hair. Very nice." Felice turned around to see a tall, powerful-looking, whiter, older version of Adrienne, wearing Army camouflage pants and a paint-covered work shirt. Her blond hair was nearly as short as Felice's. "You would look nice in dreads," Laura said admiringly.

"I forgot to tell you," Adrienne said to Felice. "Mom takes stepping into her house as an invitation to get in your business."

"I had dreads for a little while," said Laura.

"Really?" Felice was surprised. She wondered how a white person could have dreads.

"Hard to believe, but true," said Laura. "Kind of scary, it was. Not that I minded scaring *other* people. However, scaring oneself is another matter altogether."

Felice laughed.

"Hi, I'm Felice LeCroix." Felice's hand was enveloped in a forceful grip.

"Well-raised, too. Did you grow up here?"

"No, Mrs. Anderson. I'm fr..."

"Well, I see you have to be indoctrinated to the rules of this house," Laura interrupted. "First of all, I'm never Mrs. Anderson, I'm Laura. And if you call me *Miss* Laura, I'm going to slit my wrists, after I kill you first. I bet you call all your parents' friends 'Mister' and 'Miss,' don't you?"

"Yes Ma'am."

Laura threw up her hands. She turned to her daughter.

"I told you to train 'em before you bring 'em home!"

"Mom, I tried. Er, Laura."

Laura turned her attention back to Felice, inspecting her. "So, Felice, you were about to tell me where you grew up."

"Los Angeles."

"Southern Cal. You don't seem like you're from there: too normal, too polite, too much clothing."

"You sound like you've spent some time there...Laura."

"Oh, yes, in the infamous sixties. That's where I met Adrienne's father. I've also been back a time or two, doing shows."

"Laura's an artist. A pretty successful one," added Adrienne.

"Come on out back, girls. I was out there working."

Felice followed the two through the huge kitchen and out to a covered patio, where the fifty-degree, sunny day felt exceptionally warm. Their backyard was beautiful and as varied with plant life, as the living room had been varied in art. There were lilies and rose bushes, banzai trees peach trees, and plants that Felice didn't know the name of. She hadn't seen so much green since she had come to New Mexico.

"You have a nice house and a nice yard," she said to Laura.

"Thank you. I bet I know what you're thinking, though. Everything's pretty eclectic. I believe in that."

"Well, that's obvious." Felice winced at her own bluntness, but Adrienne and Laura only laughed.

"Don't fret," said Laura. "I can't stand people who mince words." She was working on a portrait of an old man. "If you want some tea or juice or something, you saw where the refrigerator is. The glasses are on the upper, middle shelf on the left side of the sink."

"No, thanks. I drank a lot of water earlier on the way up here, so I'm fine."

"Okay. Have a seat and talk to me while I work. That's the advantage of being an artist. You can work and socialize at the same time. At least I can." Laura picked up her palette from its stand and began to work on her creation.

Felice looked at the furniture. Instead of standard patio fare, Laura had placed several upright futons on her patio. The cushions, however, were upholstered with standard, weather-proof patio fabric. Felice sat.

"So, do you have a boyfriend?" asked Laura. Felice looked at Adrienne who was sitting on another futon. Adrienne just shrugged her shoulders. *I told you so.*

Felice looked at Laura's back. "No I don't."

"An attractive girl like you probably has a lot of guys chasing her."

"Not really."

"Of course with that situation you were involved in with the Taus, your social life has probably diminished somewhat."

Felice whipped her head around at Adrienne, who now held her own head in both hands. Her mother had promised that, when she met Felice, she wouldn't mention that she knew about Felice's problem. Adrienne should have known better.

"Well, I...uh...yes, yes it has."

"Sorry, Felice." Laura turned from her canvas. "My daughter tells me everything. Mostly because she knows that I am the all-wise sage who has the answer to all the problems that exist in the world." Laura flashed Felice a beatific smile. "I suppose I should thank you for coming to Adrienne's aid at the expense of your reputation. Thank you, child."

She put the palette down, came over, picked Felice up from the futon and gave her a hug. Felice was startled at first. Then she smiled and hugged the woman back. Somehow, she didn't seem so angry at Adrienne anymore. It seemed as though touching Laura had a calming affect on her. It was like hugging Grandma Anna.

"I forgot to tell you that too," said Adrienne. "If Laura likes you, you automatically become one of the family. If she doesn't, she'll put you out and warn you never to darken her door again. I'd say she likes you."

"Thank you, daughter dearest, for explaining the enigma that is me," Laura said sardonically as she released Felice.

"So, your name is mud now, at least among black people, right?"

"Yes."

"But you didn't run away. That shows some character. I'll assume that your parents know nothing about this."

"No!" Felice shuddered at the thought.

Laura laughed. "Afraid your father will go up to that place and defend your honor?"

"Exactly right," Felice said.

"Well, you're probably right, especially since you know the man and I don't. I bet you thought of quitting school, too. But, you're still there...impressive."

"Thank you."

"Have you thought of getting some vengeance for your lost reputation?"

"Actually, no. I figure it would just make things worse. Then they'd get back at me, and then I'd do the same. I'd just like it to be over."

"The vicious circle. You're right about that, at least if you were to employ most conventional forms of vengeance. But, there's a way you can get your revenge without them being able to do anything about it. A very simple method."

"How?"

Laura's back was turned again. She was putting the finishing touches on the weather-worn hat on the man's head.

"By being successful in any undertaking placed before you and by embracing love," she said almost absently.

"I tried that once and it backfired on me..."

"Yes. Daniel, wasn't it? Adrienne told me the story. However, when I mention love, the word 'trust' is implicit in it. I find it almost superfluous to say when I speak of love. Did you trust Daniel? Did you tell him about yourself?"

Felice didn't answer at first. Laura turned to her, looking at her patiently.

Finally Felice understood. "I have to say no. If I had, I would have told him about what I had done."

"Give this student an 'A.'" She turned back to her canvas. "You didn't love him and you knew instinctively that he didn't love you. So, you kept an integral part of yourself away from him, believing that if he saw it, he'd run away. How did he break it off?"

Felice looked at Adrienne. "So you didn't tell her about this, eh?"

"I thought it would be a more interesting story if it came from you," she replied.

Felice turned to Laura's back. "He had a naked girl in his room at a time when he knew that I would visit."

"Sadism, instead of love. It was a white girl, undoubtedly."

Felice shifted uncomfortably. "Yes."

Laura turned to her again. "That would be one of the most painful ways for a black man to hurt a black woman, of course."

Felice's surprise was evident. Who was this woman?

"Don't worry, child," Laura continued. "I know you and most others think of me as a white woman. But, I've had nearly twenty years of being the mother of a black child to think about this subject."

Laura continued. "Did you know that appellations 'black' and 'white' are artificial and were created to justify and facilitate slavery and imperialism? Before that dubious undertaking, there was no such thing as race. To use the word 'race' implies that you and I are of different species. It also gives the implication that one of the species is superior to the other. From this, all sorts of things have arisen, most of which you know about, undoubtedly."

Adrienne, who had heard this story before, knew that the history lesson was on its way. "I'll get us something to drink, in case you change your mind, Felice," she said as she got up. She went into the kitchen.

"When the Europeans recognized that the Africans' genes were dominant," Laura began, "they became fearful of being genetically annihilated. And since men generally initiate sexual contact, they demonized the African man, turning him into the mythical, archetypal rapist all of us nice white girls grow up hearing about. White womanhood became a thing to be glorified, cherished, and protected, especially from the inferior, evil black rampaging beast. White women eventually came to be considered the most beautiful, desirable women on the planet because of this. Conversely, her most polar physical opposite, the black woman, became the counterpart of the black man: beastly, doltish, and utterly lacking in what was (and still is) considered the most treasured quality in a woman: physical beauty.

"Human nature, such as it is, is pretty predictable. When one is told that one can't have something, one always wants that thing. White women, having heard about the sexual prowess of the black man, have lusted after them ever since. I should know," she chuckled.

Felice sat rapt.

"For their part," Laura continued, "black men have been told that the white man's 'prize,' his woman, was strictly off limits, enforced under the threat of a brutal, humiliating death. If a prize is so wonderful, however, death might be a small price to pay for acquiring it. Probably many black men unconsciously think this way. Additionally, should a black man acquire his nemesis' prize, it would serve his vengeance in a most effective way.

"What the black man didn't take into account was how his pursuit of the white woman would hurt the black woman. Having been told constantly that she is ugly--especially if she looks more African--is an affirmation of all her worst fears. This is especially true, when a black man chooses a white woman as a mate, or even as just a bed partner."

"Yes," Felice whispered.

"So, this all comes back to Daniel. I said that the black man didn't take into account the side effect of what his was doing, but that was in the past. These days, most black men *do* know how much it hurts black women when he is seen with a white woman. Either he doesn't care, or he's doing it specifically to hurt all black women, or one black woman in particular. Daniel did care."

"I knew he did it to hurt me, but I hadn't thought it out quite that far," Felice said. "I had been trying to avoid thinking about it."

"Understandable. I doubt if he thought it out so thoroughly, also."

Adrienne walked back out carrying a tray. It held three glasses and a pitcher of lemonade. She set it down on the table next to Felice.

"Oh how ante-bellum of you, my darling daughter," Laura grinned at her. Adrienne rolled her eyes as she sat back down.

"Tired of the sermon yet?" Adrienne asked Felice.

"Not at all."

"Adrienne finds this topic boring. She calls it 'amateur race psychology.'"

"Laura, don't talk about me like I'm not here. I don't think the topic is boring. It's just that you've inundated me with it for years. I don't feel the need to sit through the whole thing when you give 'the lecture' to somebody else. I brought Felice to hear it because I thought it might help."

"Am I being over sensitive?" Laura asked her daughter.

"Yes, but that's who you are-sensitive. Continue lecture."

Laura bowed to her daughter. "Thank you. Now where were we? Oh yes, Daniel. At the risk of sounding like I'm blaming the victim, I have to say this: you gave Daniel fear instead of love. You feared what Daniel would think about you if he had known the truth. Daniel found out that you didn't trust him and he was hurt by it. He had to find out about your 'reputation' from the very men who had helped you to forge it--men he probably didn't even like in the first place. It must have been quite humiliating for him, knowing what I do about the male ego."

Felice considered this. She hadn't thought about Daniel's feelings at all.

Laura turned toward her canvas again. Felice looked at the portrait, which Laura appeared to be painting from memory. On first glance, the man appeared to be past sixty, but on further inspection, Felice could see that this was not so. He was a young white man, aged beyond his years. His gray eyes appeared to be old and young at the same time. His hands were gnarled, but not spotted. His back was straight. Felice marveled at Laura's ability to capture this quality in a two-dimensional setting.

"Maybe, in a few months or so, I'll apologize to him," Felice said, almost to herself.

"That might be pushing it a bit. After all, you didn't set out to hurt him, but he certainly set out to hurt you," said Adrienne.

"Maybe you should," said Laura. "Not now, but sometime in the future, when he's able to hear it. Hopefully, he'll do the same, but don't do it just for his forgiveness."

"No...I'd do it in order to...get some peace for myself, or something like it."

"Give the student another 'A,'" said Laura quietly.

Felice smiled.

"I hope you'll think about what I've said. All of it." Laura paused for a beat. "What do you think of my work?"

"It's great."

"How so? And, no, I'm not fishing. I'd like an honest appraisal."

"Well, I'm not an expert on art or anything else, for that matter."

"Yes, you are an art expert. We all are. Either art touches something in us or we're indifferent to it, which doesn't necessarily make it bad, though sometimes it does," she smirked. "I'm asking if it touches something in you."

Felice studied the canvas again. "I like the way the man's face looks: happy and sad at the same time-kind of like me."

"And like everyone else, though we don't all realize it. High praise, indeed. Thank you, child."

Adrienne was silent. She recognized the painting as a replica of a photo of her own grandfather, a man she had never met.

* * *

The next afternoon, Felice headed toward the gym. She had been searching for Adrienne all day, suspecting that her friend had been avoiding her. She had finally found her at the one place she knew Adrienne would probably be. In the off season, about three times a week, the varsity basketball players regularly played pick-up games in the historically-preserved old gym, which was the only athletic facility still located on the campus proper. The games were heated, fierce, and coed.

She looked around at the spectators as she walked into the gym. Both the men's and women's teams had been nationally-ranked the previous season, so the pick-up games always drew a good-sized audience. To her dismay, but not unexpectedly, she spotted a number of the Taus immediately. They had spotted her as well and turned in her direction, actually pointing at her, smirking and laughing. Several of their female friends and sorority sisters, the Tau Lambda Pi, eyed her with scorn. She had been invited to pledge Tau Lambda at the beginning of her freshman year, but now none of the sorority sisters would be caught dead even talking to her. During a break in the action, even a couple of the male players eyed her with smirks on their faces.

So she set herself down, alone at the end of one of the bleachers, trying to block out everything but the game.

There was Adrienne, sure enough, getting back on defense. Each team was as evenly mixed gender-wise as possibly. On Adrienne's team, there were two women and three men; on the other, the ratio was reversed. Felice grinned as she watched Adrienne, hair tied back, yank down a defensive rebound over a male player who was at least three inches taller. Adrienne, one of the few women who could palm a basketball, shot an outlet pass to Jerome Moore, the starting center of NMU's men's varsity team. Seven-feet tall, but surprisingly graceful, he dribbled the ball

for a few seconds. Then he pulled up for a baseline jumper.
The ball encircled the rim and then bounced out. But then
who should get the rebound, but Adrienne? She had raced
up court and was now underneath the opposing goal. Felice
grinned as her friend yanked down yet another rebound and,
after ducking under a defender, put up a baby hook shot.
Swish! All net.

Some of the Taus looked over at Felice in scorn, as
they watched her jump up and cheer.

"You go, girl!" she shouted.

"Look at that. She doesn't even have the decency to
keep a low profile," Kim Adams said to Vonetta Hall. "If I
were her, I would have transferred to another school or
dropped out."

Vonetta said nothing as Kim went on ripping into
Felice. Vonetta had once thought of Felice as her little sister,
but when she found out what Felice had done, she had to
restrain herself from strangling her.

Now, she wasn't sure how she felt about her. Calvin
had come back to her, professing his love, and begging her
forgiveness, and after a time, she had let him back into her
life.

She looked over at Felice. Felice had hurt and betrayed her, and for a little while after that, Vonetta had been so bitter and cynical, she had wondered if it were possible to trust anyone again. But now, she and Calvin were back together, and her life pretty much continued on the course it had been before.

Vonetta was happy that she had been mature enough not to have exacted some kind of revenge on Felice. She thought back to when she had been a sixteen-year-old gang member in Chicago. Had something like this happened then, Vonetta would have gotten her girls together and they would have made Felice wish she had never been born. But, that was another life.

Vengeance is mine, sayeth the Lord and, boy, wasn't that right? She had known about Felice's other escapades and had warned her to be careful. But, Felice hadn't listened and had paid the price. Now Felice sat alone, vilified, and shunned by nearly every black person on campus. Vonetta had tried hard to feel happy that Felice had gotten her comeuppance, but, somehow, could not.

"Why doesn't that ho just sit down?" Kim's contemptuous voice sounded in her ears.

"Can we talk about something else? The last person I want to talk about is Felice LeCroix."

"Oh, sorry, girl. I understand. You must really hate her."

Vonetta silently looked over at her former friend again, feeling nothing in her heart but pity.

"Oh, *that's* the one. I might have to get me some of that," said the new Tau Sigma pledge, Kwame Lewis, to his 'big brother,' Andre Carter. "Kinda skinny, but look at that ass!"

"Yeah, she likes us Taus, but 'big brothers' have first dibs," grinned Andre. "Besides, a hoochie like that might shoot you down. Trevor and them said they all used condoms, but who knows who else has been there? She might have HIV, THC, and M-O-U-S-E, for all anybody knows." They both laughed.

"Who's she cheering for?"

"That nappy-headed, yellow bitch, Adrienne Anderson," sneered Andre, pointing at the court, his pride still smarting from their encounter. "That's the skank who yaps on and on about the Greeks. Those two are real tight. Hey, maybe they've turned into labia-lappers!"

"Could be. When I was in high school, the girls' entire basketball team was dykes."

Andre's mind churned with malice, an idea for the perfect revenge forming in his mind. So Felice thought she was too good for him, did she? So she thought he was a bastard, did she? So that big, half-white bitch Adrienne was going to beat him down, was she? Well, let's see how they both liked the latest about them. They thought they were so smart. He'd make their lives so miserable that they'd never want to set foot on this campus again.

"So, how come you didn't tell your mom about Kevin? You seemed to have told her everything else about me," said Felice looking at Adrienne, unable to decide if she were angry or not.

They sat on the bleachers as the gym emptied out. Adrienne's team had won this round, with Adrienne scoring fifteen points and yanking down ten rebounds. Several of the players on each team slapped her high-five and on the shoulders as they walked by. "Good game," they all said, eyeing Felice curiously.

Tale of the Tigers

Adrienne looked at her sheepishly, toweling the sweat from her forehead. "I'm sorry. But I knew Mom could help. Believe me; I haven't breathed a word to anyone else."

"Well, it's not like everyone else doesn't know almost everything already," Felice sighed. "But you must have been feeling guilty, since you've been hiding from me all day. Made me have to come up in here and deal with almost every Negro on campus looking at me like I have leprosy."

"Sorry. "

Felice thought for a minute. "Actually, there's something fun about being a social outcast. Everybody leaves you alone." Felice grinned. "And gets upset when you're happy. When you tossed up that hook, I jumped up and cheered."

"Yeah, I heard your big mouth."

"When I sat back down, I noticed that some of 'em were looking at me like I lost my mind."

"What did Laura say? Something about happiness being the best revenge?"

"It looks that way, doesn't it? You didn't answer my question."

"Why didn't I tell her about Kevin? Laura can't stand most white men. She would have been more against it than

I am. Remember what I told you the other day about white men? Where do you think I got all that propaganda from?" she giggled.

"Too weird: a white woman, with a half-black daughter, being against me dating a white man."

"Yeah, I know."

"So, you still think it's not a good idea?"

"Yes. No. Heck, I don't know."

"I saw him on Saturday."

"What?"

"I accidentally ran into him in the mall when I was looking for a birthday present for my dad." Felice told her the whole story.

"Wow! Already had that first date. So what do you think? Anything happening?"

"Possibly."

"Have you seen him today?"

"No. Maybe he's hiding from me, too."

"From what you told me, I doubt it. Why didn't you give him your phone number?"

"Do you know what my dad told me when I was about fifteen? He said that I better not ever embarrass him by having a white man coming to his door asking for his daughter."

"Uh-oh! So, you gonna to see him on the sly?"

"That would be a definite 'no.' I've had enough of hiding things from my folks and from everybody else. It takes too much energy to lie."

"So, you gonna to give him the brush-off?"

"I don't know."

Adrienne looked at her. "Please! You know you're going to go for it and why not? Don't you think you've had a crappy enough time around this joint already? Whatever mistakes you've made, you've paid for them. It's time for you to have some fun and to hell with what Laura, your dad, and especially these idiots around here think. Go out with him again. If somebody around here doesn't like it, tell 'em to kiss your ass!"

"A little steamed, aren't we? Since you know so much, tell me what to do about my dad."

"Does your mom feel the same way?"

"I'm not sure, but I kind of don't think so. She's always been much more tolerant than Dad."

"She might be on your side."

"I'd hate to put them in that position."

"Well, girl, then you have to decide whether it's worth it or not. Look, I've got to get a shower."

Felice waved her hand in front of her face. "I thought something was kickin'."

"Keep on, hear? I'll call you later."

Chapter Four

"The Supreme Court makes most of its decisions based on *stare decisis*. That is to say, it makes its decisions following those principles of law that have been established in similar cases that have been decided earlier."

Mr. Weinberg, Felice's political science professor, had a habit of speaking in long, run-on sentences. This posed a problem for some students, but she wasn't one of them. She had the useful ability to pick out pertinent information from whatever topic any professor lectured. She found the workings of the Supreme Court particularly fascinating; its schedule, its procedures, its history. She, for one, had no idea (until now), that the court based all of its decisions solely on a case's compatibility with the U.S. Constitution. How odd, she now thought, to be born and grow up in a country with a two hundred year-old Constitution and barely know anything about it.

"However, on occasion, the court will rule against *stare decisis* if it deems that a prior court's decision in the pertinent case was misinterpreted, i.e., wrong, and/or in conflict with the content or the spirit of the Constitution. Such was the case in *Brown v. Board of Education*, decided in 1955. The decision in this case struck down that of a prior court's case, *Plessy v. Ferguson*, 1896. We'll discuss the two cases on Friday. See you then."

The subject of government had not been one of Felice's strong suits in high school, mostly due to her overall boredom with school, rather than lack of aptitude. But now, after taking one of the general education requirements for graduation, Political Science, she found herself enthralled. Her professor was a middle-aged man who had a reputation for being a taskmaster. When she had told another student who her instructor was, he had advised her to take one of the other political science classes, one with an easier teacher.

The advice had intrigued her: a challenge? So she had stayed in the class and, so far, was happy she did. Most of the instructions up to that point leaned heavily on the content and workings of the Constitution. It was such a short, simple document, but with so much meaning. All the duties of each branch of the government laid out in perfect clarity, with no branch having precedence over the other and each having power to keep the other two in check. It wasn't a perfect document and its framers knew it could never possibly be, so they gave future lawmakers the power to change it with the ever-changing spirit of the times. Felice was fascinated.

The articles and amendments of the Constitution began to swirl through Felice's head as she gathered her belongings. Mr. Weinberg had required that each student read the Constitution--which was in the front of the textbook--in its entirety at least once a week, and Felice, for the most part, complied. One particular part of the first article stayed with her: the passage on taxation and representation.

"...which shall be determined by adding to the whole Number of free Persons, including those bound to Service for a

Term of Years, and excluding Indians not taxed, three fifths of all other Persons."

All other persons...meaning slaves...meaning her ancestors. She vaguely remembered hearing of the 'three-fifths' part of the Constitution, but hadn't known exactly what it meant, nor had she grasped its significance until now. She now recalled hearing one of her father's militant L.A. friends railing about how blacks had been considered three-fifths of a human being by the nation's Founding Fathers, but she now wondered if that man had really known what he was talking about—if he had really grasped the significance of that part of the Constitution beyond the surface insult.

According to her textbook and one of Mr. Weinberg's previous lectures, during the formation of the U.S., the Founding Fathers decided that the number of congressmen from each state sent to the House of Representatives would be decided by each state's population. The southern slave-holding states had been so concerned that they would be dominated by the northern non-slave-holding states, due to the latter's superior numbers, that they threatened to pull away from the northern states and form their own nation. In order to prevent this, a compromise was struck. Each slave would be counted as three-fifths of a person, in order to bolster the southern states' representation in the House of Representatives, in order to get the South to join the Union.

But, in the Declaration of Independence, didn't Thomas Jefferson claim that all men had God-given rights such as life, liberty, and the pursuit of happiness? The hypocrisy, especially that of the northern states, screamed at her, as if the Constitution had only recently been drafted. The northern states compromised only because they needed the southern states' agricultural products. Not only had the slaves been given only partial representation only when it served the white southerners' purposes, but they had not been given a voice. That definitely didn't suit the slaveholders' purposes. At least they had the decency not to tax the non-represented Natives, but she then wondered whether it was decency or expediency. It would have been kind of hard to go get those taxes. Then she remembered that the Natives were not considered citizens.

But a thought occurred to her out of the blue: what would have happened if the North had told the South that it could not join the Union? What would the course of history looked like under *those* circumstances? As Felice walked into the Quad, she imagined herself walking in chains.

After slavery, blacks were recognized as full citizens and the three-fifths clause became irrelevant. However, the South wasn't having any of it and it continued to ignore Thomas Jefferson's assertions about God and man, culminating in *Plessy v. Ferguson*. Felice remembered learning about Reconstruction and Jim Crow in an earlier history class, one of the few times she had paid attention to her high school studies. It had seemed to her that many white people loathed black people and loved them at the same time. They loathed/loved them because they needed to have someone be lower than they. This schizophrenia was demonstrated many years later in the era of Marcus Garvey. He had wanted to take all black Americans Back-to-Africa from which their ancestors had been kidnapped. Felice wondered whether she would have been a part of that movement had she lived in that day. After all, judging by white America's treatment of black Americans up to that point in time, she would have thought that this was what most of the white Americans had wanted as well. However, Garvey's back-to-Africa organization, the Afro-American Improvement Association, was undermined by government plants, and Garvey, a Jamaican by birth, was deported.

What did this mean? How was she to judge this history, along with the subsequent seventy years?

She got into the cafeteria line to order herself a breakfast sandwich and orange juice. After doing so, she turned and looked around at the mass of tables in the cafeteria, which were filled nearly to capacity. There were smatterings of black students, but only one or two, and not as many Latinos as one might expect at a major university in the southwestern United States. Most of the heads of hair were straight and blond, red, or light brown. She wondered if any of them had any concept of the dual nature of this country. Probably not, and if they did, they would probably ignore it. She considered the black students-bet many of them didn't have a clue either. A generation ago, back when Joseph LeCroix was eating breakfast here maybe, but now, forget it.

It occurred to her, as she paid for her breakfast, that black people had mimicked white peoples' love/loath conundrum. They loved/loathed white people and loved/loathed themselves. Look at the color thing. Felice couldn't count the times she had been called black and ugly as a child. Nor could she count the times that, as a young woman, she had been told that she was pretty, to be so dark.

She remembered seeing the movie *School Daze*. So many black people got mad at how Spike Lee had aired their dirty laundry. Others had even denied that such situations existed. Talk about denying reality! She remembered how one girl in high school said, upon seeing her light-skinned father, "you don't look anything like him. He's so handsome." She remembered how her own grandmother-- her father's mother--reacted when she stopped straightening her hair. "You look just like those nappy-headed Africans now," she had said, as if it were the worst insult in the world. She thought of the Taus and how they railed against white people in general, but only a few of them had a steady girlfriend who was black.

The thought sent a wave of guilt through her as she sat down at one of the few empty tables in the Quad. One of the Taus she had slept with, had been the ex-boyfriend of a girl, who used to be a friend of hers. That friendship had ended upon exposure of Felice's deeds. Vonetta was older than most of the students at the university; about twenty- five. She had worked with Felice in the African Cultural Center during the summer and had taken the younger woman under her wing. She had been having a few problems with her boyfriend, Calvin--a Tau fraternity brother five years her junior--and would occasionally confide in Felice about them. After the two had broken up, Calvin began to pursue Felice. Felice had, by then, had fleeting relationships with Trevor, the fraternity's president and another Tau, but, stupidly, didn't take this or his prior relationship with her friend into consideration at all. All she saw was Calvin. He wasn't overly handsome, but was the nicest and smartest of any of the Taus she had come into contact with. She had liked him a lot and had naively thought that they would be able to keep their relationship a secret. Calvin, however, still had feelings for Vonetta, and had broken off his relationship with Felice after only a month and a half.

Now, she thought of nothing but remorse. Vonetta had been her friend and how had she repaid that friendship? Laura had asked her why she hadn't thought of revenge. The secret was that she deserved no revenge. *Had Vonetta been another kind of woman*, she thought, *I'd have been in the hospital at the start of the fall semester.*

Felice sighed. Laura and Adrienne might think that she was a victimized innocent in this whole situation, but she knew better. She had callously stabbed Vonetta straight in the back and for what reason? Thoughtlessness?

Whorishness? Stupidity? Hatred? Did she hate Vonetta or the Taus or herself? Did she hate all black people? Was this a part of the love/loath relationship that black people have with each other? Felice's head was beginning to ache.

"Hi."

Felice looked up into Kevin's smiling face. He was holding a bagel and some kind of sports drink. "Mind if I sit down? There's not a lot of room in here."

"Go ahead," she gestured. "Though I'm sure that most of the people in here wouldn't mind if you sat with them. You're famous, remember?"

"Don't remind me. The question is whether I want to sit with them."

"Spoken like a big-time athlete."

"Who can't get his head through any doorway." He tentatively sat, then looked at her.

"Are you sure you don't mind? You looked like you were untangling the problems of the western world just now."

"Go ahead. The western world can wait, believe me."

"Okay. So how was the rest of your weekend?'

"Not bad. I had lunch at my friend's house in Santa Fe on Sunday. Her mother is an artist and they have an interesting house. Her mother is...different...a good different."

"Still eating, I see," he said with a grin.

Felice shot him a mock threatening look. "Man must eat to live. Woman, too, pal." She eyed his bagel.

"Mine!" He said, encircling his arms around his food. Felice mimed, throwing her fork at him, as they both laughed. Just then, a blond young woman that Felice didn't know passed them, barely noticing them. However, familiar laughter caught the woman's attention and she turned around. Felice saw her mouth fall open a little then heard it lightly snap shut. It was one of the girls that had been with Kevin on that day he had first spoken to her in the Quad lounge--the same one he had told to shut up.

The woman quickly recovered her aplomb as she came back to their table. Since she was approaching from Kevin's back, he couldn't see the green daggers that were her eyes.

"Hi, Kevin," Felice heard the woman say sweetly. Her smile was wide as she came around to the side of the table. The green daggers were gone. Apparently, they were only for Felice.

"Oh, hi Mandy," he said. Felice could almost sense the woman's fear at the nonchalance in Kevin's voice.

"I thought we were supposed to have a tutoring session today."

"Oh, sorry, I got to talking with Felice, here, and, uh...do you know each other?"

"No." Try as she might, Mandy couldn't keep the sarcasm out of that one word.

Kevin appeared to not have heard the tone. "Mandy, this is Felice; Felice, Mandy."

"Hi," said both women. Felice gave Mandy a close-lipped smile and held out her hand. For a fraction of a second, Felice could see Mandy inspecting her hand, as if for cleanliness. Then she shook it.

What a light, limp-wristed handshake that was, Felice thought, mentally comparing it to Laura Anderson's.

"Pleased to meet you," said Mandy. The sweetness in her voice did reach her eyes, however.

"I guess we'll have to skip this session," said Kevin. "Let's meet in the lounge on Friday, okay?"

Mandy looked as if she were about to plead with Kevin, then she thought better of it. "Okay, honey. I'll see you later then," she purred, stroking his shoulder seductively. "Bye." She kissed him on the cheek and sauntered away.

Felice's eyebrows had shot up at the kiss. "Your girlfriend?" she asked casually; slightly amused; indifferently.

"That would be a 'no.'" Kevin's face, which had reddened considerably when Mandy kissed him, was now only a medium pink.

"Well, apparently she's something to you."

"Yes, she is. She's my tutor and my friend, and that's it."

"Oh. That's good."

"Really?"

"Yes. It's just that I don't want her to have a fit every time she sees me talking to you."

"So, you anticipate that we might talk to each other again in the future?"

"Maybe...after all, how can I not talk to a man who bought me a double-combo plate at a nice Mexican restaurant?"

"A girl who likes to eat-ahh, how refreshing! What other kinds of food do you like?"

"Italian, German, Chinese, Japanese, Creole, of course...though with my parents' restaurant, The Creole

Experience, I'm about burnt out on the Creole. What about you?"

"All of the above plus Greek; ever had it?"

"No. But I heard it's good; according to my dad, at least, who's tasted just about any kind of food you can imagine."

"So, you come by your appetite honestly."

Felice looked a little hurt.

"No, no. I like watching you eat. I like a girl who can put it away. It shows a love of the good things in life."

"The good things?"

"Yes, the good things. Things like good food, good drink, fun, laughter, love...the good things; the things that make it fun to be alive."

"Oh...thanks."

"You're welcome."

"But, you know what they say. Too much of a good thing can be a bad thing."

"Who is this 'they' anyway and why is it that 'they' always have something to say?"

"Good point." She smiled at him. "Maybe 'they' should get a life of their own and stay out of yours and mine."

"Good point."

A few minutes later, Kevin was walking Felice to her World Lit class. As usual, he was greeted by nearly everyone they passed, most of them eyeing Felice as they spoke. Hardly, anyone said hello to Felice, however.

"Do you have many friends?" he asked.

"No-just one." She paused. "It's pretty much been that way most of my life. I guess I'm not the most sociable person in the world."

"You're probably better off. I don't have too many friends, either."

"It seems like you do from here."

"Those aren't friends. Those are associates, hangers-on, groupies and the like."

"That sounds pretty harsh."

"Harsh, but true; Malik is the only person around here that I consider an actual friend. Pretty strange considering how different we are."

"Different how?-besides the obvious."

"Well, he's from a big city, Detroit, and I'm from here. He grew up poor and I didn't. He's smart and I'm not."

"He's got a harem and you've got a harem."

"And what is that supposed to mean?"

"Usually when I see you...either one of you, there's a gaggle of girls around. You must have given them the slip when you sat down with me."

"True enough. Those are the groupies. That's what I'm talking about: the difference between liking me because I'm a football star, and liking me because I'm a great guy. My friends like me because I'm a great guy!"

"You only have one friend, so you must not be that great of a guy," she teased.

He put his hand to his heart and pretended to look hurt. "Oh Miss LeCroix you have wounded me grievously!"

She laughed as they approached her class.

"Well, here it is." She suddenly grew serious. "Kevin."

He warmed at the sound of her speaking his name. "Yes?"

She looked at him sadly. "I only have one friend because I'm really not that great of a girl. I'll see you around." She turned and headed toward her classroom.

Kevin, frozen for a moment, watched her retreating back. Then he sprinted, easily overtaking her and blocking her path.

"Wait! I'd like to call you sometime. Maybe we can try that Greek stuff or maybe go bike-riding."

She looked at him with amazement. "What do they call this-class interference?"

"Good one...corny...but good. Actually, it's called brush-off interference."

"555-9087. Bye." She hurried away.

He threw off his backpack, immediately pulled a pen and a sheet of paper out of it, and scribbled the number down. He looked up just barely in time to see her going through the doorway of the classroom. She was smiling at him.

* * *

In her dormitory room, Amanda Bain, known as "Mandy" to all except her mother, stood in front of her mirror, staring at her own bloodshot eyes. She had been crying. All of her hopes for her and Kevin were gone, dashed away by...by some mousy black girl. How? How had it happened? She had been a good friend to Kevin, though she hadn't been interested in more than that, at least at first. But after they had studied many times together, laughed and joked together, talked about politics, religion and the weather together, she had thought, "maybe." After he started frequently telling her how smart and wonderful and lovely and good to talk to she was, she began to think he was interested in her, and began to think, "maybe, just maybe."

Then, an unwelcome scene intruded on her reverie. Kevin had told her to shut up the other day just so he could say hello to that girl. She tried to banish the scene but it wouldn't go away. Seeing the two of them together, not long after he had shushed her to speak to that girl, had struck fear in her heart. She hadn't meant to give the girl the evil eye, but she couldn't help herself. When she had seen the two of them sitting there laughing like the friends that Mandy and Kevin *really were*, it was like a kick in the stomach. She knew what was happening, but she couldn't understand it. Her mother had always told her, that to be a good woman to a man, you first had to be his friend. That's what she had tried to do with Kevin, and Mandy doubted that he had ever even spoken to this girl before the Quad incident.

Mandy had grown up in a family where black people had been tolerated, but looked down upon. There was a large part of her that knew this was wrong and racist, but then there was that other part, that ugly part of Mandy, that felt that Felice was beneath her. Not only was Felice beneath her, but Kevin had known nothing about her. What could he possibly want with *her*? All he seemed to know about her was that she was...beautiful. Unfortunately, Mandy could not deny it. And then she was shy and quiet--totally different from Mandy in all respects. Mandy was headstrong, talkative and wasn't shy about demonstrating her intellect and knowledge. Nor was she shy about letting someone know when they patronized her.

Kevin had done that just once. Mandy also recognized that Kevin was smart and there was one particular subject that he knew a lot about...math. During the math class in which they were both enrolled, she had to him to ask for his guidance about a problem. Instead of answering her question, however, he had treated her as if she were an idiot, seeming to forget that she had guided him through Political Science and English. He went all the way back to the beginning of the class, as if she had been sleeping in class from day one. She felt as though he were treating her as if she were stupid. When she got angry with him and told him about it, he simply walked away from her.

But after a few days, they were talking again. Mandy was the type who might get angry at someone, but if she really thought that person was her friend, she'd forget about it. When they started talking again, the argument never came up and she thought everything was all right.

Now, she wondered how much of her natural forthrightness was what had driven Kevin away, and had driven him toward someone like...what was her name...Felice. She had seen Felice a couple of times around campus. She was nearly always alone, never talking to anyone, never hanging out in a pack of girls, and never loud and boisterous like she noticed that some black girls were.

Mandy knew that there were parts of her personality that had probably driven Kevin away. She was a tough, no-nonsense kind of girl, even with him. And she didn't change, even when she had begun to develop feelings for him. But she wouldn't patronize him, in spite of, or, rather, because of this. She didn't really know how to be submissive. Every time she had tried, it felt fake to her.

Mandy's mother, having been abandoned by her husband when Mandy was a toddler, told her that a woman had to be tough, had to speak her mind, and let a man know *who* she was.

Mandy knew that some men wanted their women to defer to them, but wondered how much of this was deferral and how much it was "just getting along." Kevin had never accused her of being hard to get along with, but other guys had. She began inspecting herself closer in the mirror, running her hands through her shoulder length hair.

"Here I am," she said to the mirror. "I'm blonde; I'm green-eyed. Many men are attracted to me—at first, anyway. But, Kevin went for someone totally opposite from me in looks and in bearing. What was that?"

She looked at the mirror defiantly. "I'm me. If Kevin doesn't like me-the real me—then maybe I didn't belong with him in the first place.

"But I know how I felt...feel, about him, and not just because he's the star player of the Tigers. He's smart, generous, funny, and has the qualities that the love of a good woman would bring out."

Sadly, she realized, however, that it wasn't *her* love that he wanted. And no amount of insight or wishing could change that. She put her head on her arms and sobbed.

Did she really love him? Did she know how to love him or anyone else? She didn't know the answers to those questions. There was only one person she knew to ask and it wasn't her mother. For the first time, since she was a child, she found herself praying.

Chapter Five

On Thursday evening, Felice was sitting alone at her kitchen table, going over her German, one of the courses she had to repeat. Initially, she had been intimidated by its alien syntax and sounds. However, she was now finding that if she opened her mind to it, the knowledge came. It wasn't English, she constantly reminded herself. So, the mind had to be set into that of a child, because as far as this language was concerned, she was a child again.

She heard her front door open and looked at the clock hanging over the stove. That would be Mom, bringing Joey back from school. Sure enough, she heard the chattering of her eight-year-old brother, telling their mother about his day. He bounded into the kitchen, which of late, was his favorite place. On seeing his sister, he ran up to her.

"Hi, Fleece! Guess what I did today?

"Hi, Junebug! Let's see...you hit a homer at little league, right?"

"Better than that, I struck out Pete!" Peter Garcia was Joey's best friend and their team's most prolific hitter.

Vetra, following her son into the kitchen, interrupted. "Don't call him Junebug. You know how much I hate that."

"Well, Mom," Felice grinned, "You remember I told you not to name him after Dad because people would call him that or 'Little Joe.' Imagine if you had named me 'Vetra.' I'd be called 'Little Vetra' to this day."

Her mother cringed. "Point taken. Well, you know that it was you father's idea."

"Yeah, blame it on Dad." She smiled at her mother. "I thought you ran things around here." Vetra gave her a mock-threatening look. "Besides," Felice continued, turning to tease her brother, "he is kind of like a bug, always under foot and everything." She began to tickle him.

"Stop it, Fleece," the boy screamed between his giggles.

* * *

Happiness filled Vetra LeCroix as she watched her children and listened to their laughter. They were so far apart in age, but very close. Felice always had time for Joey and only occasionally expressed impatience with him, which was usually justified. She studied her daughter. She had grown into an exceptionally beautiful woman, as Felice's father had pointed out a couple of days ago with some anxiety. Vetra had laughed at her husband.

"She's just like you, Joe," Vetra had said with a slanted grin.

"That's what I'm worried about." In the last few months, Vetra had sensed that something had been eating at Felice, but when Vetra tried to draw her out, she was as tight-lipped as ever. Vetra had initially thought that it was Felice's grades of the previous semester. On further reflection, however, Vetra surmised that the low grades were the symptom of a problem, not the problem itself. What that problem was, Vetra hadn't a clue and Felice wasn't telling, so Vetra had to content herself with letting Felice work it out on her own. *She plays her cards close to the vest, just like me,* thought Vetra with some admiration.

"*Eins, zwei, drei, vier, fünf...,*" she heard Felice recite.

"Eins, swi, try, fear, fuf," Joey repeated obediently.

That's my girl. Felice had always excelled at whatever she put any amount of effort into. Getting her to put some effort into something had been a major bone of contention between them, however. But this semester, for whatever reason, Felice seemed to take her education far more seriously than ever. Vetra would come home each afternoon to find Felice deep into study on any one of the subjects she was taking, and after dinner, she would be in her room at her desk, pouring over her notes so late into the night that Vetra or Joseph would have to tell her to go to bed. That had never happened before. Additionally, she would actually talk with her parents about what she had learned in those classes, with unprecedented enthusiasm. Something had lit a fire under her daughter, possibly this mysterious problem that she had. Whatever it was, Vetra had decided not to look a gift-horse in the mouth. She hoped it would last.

Vetra knew instinctively that Felice was destined for great things. For what, however, she didn't know. Her daughter had always been astonishingly intelligent, but aimless, unfocused, and searching. Her intelligence, however, had interfered with her popularity. At one of Felice's high school parent-teacher-student functions, Vetra had once watched her interact with others her own age.

During most of the gathering, Felice had stood apart from the others, wearing a look of exasperation on her face. Later, Vetra had asked her about it, but Felice had shrugged off the question.

"Mom, I just don't like that many people."

Vetra thought that Felice was only half joking. She had always only had one friend, never hanging out in a group or a pack. Lately, it was this Adrienne, a tall, mixed-raced girl, who seemed to be as much an individualist as her daughter, if those dreadlocks were any indication.

Vetra knew that the fights she and her daughter had, were often caused by her own fear: fear that Felice was too much like her. Fear that Felice would bypass opportunities; the same types of opportunities that Vetra had bypassed as a teenager. She had vowed that things would be different for her daughter, but her daughter long had refused to cooperate-until now. It looked as though God had finally answered Vetra's prayers. Still, Vetra wondered what cross Felice had to bear to get her to this point. She was sure that Felice would never tell her. Of course, it probably had something to do with the opposite sex. Felice was eighteen, after all. Still Vetra wasn't quite sure that this was the answer. Felice had never had a bunch of boys calling the house. There had been a serious one in her senior year of high school, but that had fizzled after the family moved away from California. Vetra idly wondered if her daughter was still a virgin. She hoped not, though she would never admit it to her husband—or to Felice for that matter. These were different days than those in which she had grown up. Though she, herself, had been a virgin when she got married and she had always been very happy with her husband sexually, she had occasionally wondered what other men might be like in bed. Oh, she would never dream of actually trying to find out, of course. She was merely curious. It might have been nice to experiment, just a little bit.

She hoped that Felice would experiment, just a little bit, before she picked one out. Vetra chuckled at her own thought. Her own grandmother was probably spinning in her grave.

Just as she turned to walk out of the kitchen, the telephone rang. Vetra turned back to pick up the kitchen extension.

"Hello?"

"Hello, Felice?" A male voice said.

"No. This is her mother." Felice turned to look at her.

"Oh, I'm sorry. Mrs. LeCroix, is it?"

"Yes."

"Hello, Mrs. LeCroix. My name is Kevin Hart. How are you?

"Fine, thank you.”

"That's great. May I speak to Felice, please?"

"Of course. Just one second." She put the receiver to her shoulder. "For you. Very polite, he is."

She started to hand Felice the receiver.

"I'll take it in the living room," said Felice, however, as she got up.

"Okay." Vetra put the receiver to her ear, her mind filled with a thousand waiting questions.

"Okay, Mom," sounded her daughter's voice. Vetra reluctantly hung up the receiver.

* * *

"Hello?"

"Hi, Felice. This is Kevin." *Of course I know who it is. It's not like the guys are beating down my door now.*

"Hi, Kevin," she said instead, as casually as she could muster.

"How are things?"

"Not too bad." After she said it, she realized it was true. Things were going not too badly at all. "I was in the middle of my German homework."

"Oh, I'm sorry."

"No, that's okay. My mother and my little brother had just walked in, so I was messing around with him. He's almost nine and kind of a pest, but kind of fun, too."

"Do you have any other brothers or sisters?"

"Nope. Just me and Joey. How about you?"

"Just me and nobody."

"Oh yeah, I forgot. You're an only child. Spoiled brats, all. I should know. I was one for long enough."

"You'd better believe it, girl. I'm used to getting what I want."

"Me too, pal. Though, since Joey's been around, I've had to share some attention. I tease him every Christmas, telling him that I remember the days when all the presents under the tree were just for me."

Kevin laughed. "Spoken like a true member of the Spoiled Brat Club."

"Dues-paying member. Being one as well, you probably already know that we spoiled brats get slapped down on occasion."

"Sure do. And it doesn't feel too good, either. But, the non-spoiled brats enjoy it so much I think we ought to be generous enough to let them have their way-but only once in a while."

"Agreed. So, how's your life?"

"Same slop, different day: Homework, practice, agents."

"Agents?"

"Sports agents."

"Oh, yeah."

"My dad calls them 'lizard lawyers.' I guess lawyers need somebody to look down on, since everyone else looks down on them."

"I guess they're all really looking forward to representing you next year."

"It seems so. My dad keeps 'em in check, though."

"What's your bachelor's in?"

"Business."

"Are you thinking of starting up a business while you're playing in the NFL? What kind?"

"I don't know. Maybe sporting goods or something related. What's your major?"

"I don't have one yet. I thought maybe English. But since I've been taking Political Science, I was thinking about having that as my major. I find it really interesting."

"Really?" He was intrigued. "You don't find many girls who take on heavy duty subjects like that one. Too bad, too."

"Too bad?"

"Yes. Having more women take on the political establishment in its own playing field, would infuse it with a fresh perspective--according to my dad, anyways. In plain English, I guess he means that women with brains have a tendency to shake up the old guys who think that a woman's place is in the kitchen and the bedroom."

"Nice translation. Your dad sounds like a pretty enlightened guy. What about you?"

"I do happen to like a woman who can count to ten and spell her name," he replied playfully.

"One... two...uh, three...uh...what comes after that, again?" drawled Felice in her best Valley Girl voice.

"Bye. Click."

"Fine, be that way," she laughed.

"So, are you dumb enough to go out with me to that Greek place we talked about?"

"Um, when are we talking about here?"

"Saturday."

How was she going to break this to her father and

have him calm down and accept it in such a short period of time?

"Well," he said, "how many minutes are you going to let me swing in the breeze?"

"What time?"

"How about seven thirty?"

"Okay."

"Can't pass up a good meal, right?"

"You better leave me and my appetite alone."

"I better ask my dad for his credit card."

She gave him the raspberry through the receiver.

"So, I guess if I don't see you tomorrow, I'll talk to you Saturday."

"Okay. Bye."

"Wait! It'll be kind of hard to pick you up without knowing where you live. What's your address?"

Here was the point of no return. She knew that if she gave it to him, there was no turning back. The confrontation with her father was set.

"1435 Las Palmas Southwest."

"Got it. Bye, darlin.'"

"Bye." She hung up the receiver, her ears tingling--her thoughts an exhilarating mixture of anticipation and dread.

* * *

After she replaced the receiver, Vetra had discreetly stayed in the kitchen, helping her son with one of his lessons. One part of her brain was engaged in helping her son, while another kept turning something over and over again. Kevin Hart. Why did that name seem so familiar?

Because they had been here less than three years, Vetra didn't know that many people. Maybe it was the son of one of Joseph's old teammates from college. She remembered meeting several of her husband's old friends. One of them had been a tall, handsome black man, who had mentioned that one of his sons went to NMU, but she couldn't remember his name. Wait. His name was Moore, she suddenly remembered, so it wasn't his son. Hart. For whatever reason, the name was somehow linked to the game of football in Vetra's mind.

"Mommy, who's Fleece talking to?"

Vetra's attention snapped back to her son. "That's Felice's business, not yours," she said sternly, but not angrily. "Your business is this homework, mister. What about the answer?"

"Fifty-six."

"Correct! You've pretty good at this, honey. A lot better than you think. I know you'll get an 'A.' Now let's do the next one."

Vetra heard Felice replace the receiver in the living room.

"Mommy. *You know* you want to know who Fleece was talking to!" Joey giggled at his mother.

"I already know, Mr. Nose. Next problem." Vetra's voice was again stern, but privately, she was amused. How could she blame her son for being nosy? He had come by it honestly.

***

"Mom?"

A couple of hours later, Felice tapped lightly on her mother's bedroom door, hoping that she hadn't fallen asleep. The light from one of the nightstand lamps shone under the door, but that was no guarantee that Vetra was awake. On nights when her husband worked late, Vetra would often fall asleep reading, her reading glasses still on her face, and an open book on her chest. This time, however, was different.

"Come in, honey." Felice opened the door walked, over to the bed and sat on the edge, next to her mother.

"Mom, I have a date on Saturday night to go to dinner."

"With this Kevin Hart?"

"Yes."

"He sounds like a polite young man. No 'is Felice there' or 'lemme speak to Felice' like a few of the geniuses who've called you before."

Felice laughed. Telephone etiquette was one of her mother's biggest pet peeves.

"Yes. He seems like a nice guy," Felice agreed.

"Since he told me his name, I've been trying to figure out where I've heard it before. It seems like I've met someone by that name or heard of someone with a similar name."

Felice inhaled deeply, exhaled and then spoke. "He's the quarterback of NMU's football team."

"Really? Then I must have seen him on TV while you and your father...." She trailed off, as the image of a face entered her head.

"Felice," she said as she took off her glasses. "Do you have any idea of how your father's going to react to this?"

"I have a pretty good idea. You remember what he told me about this?"

"Yes. I was so angry at him, but he wouldn't budge.

Felice, do you really want to do this?"

"Yes, Mom. I...like him and he likes me too, the *real* me, not the "me" I'm supposed to be."

Vetra looked at Felice intensely. "What do you mean?"

Felice thought for a second. "He likes me the way I am; not like I'm someone who's supposed to be an..."

"Appendage?" said Vetra knowingly.

"Exactly. So many guys act as though my whole purpose in life is to...be what they want me to be, make them look good, instead of letting me be what I want to be. Remember Tommy from my freshman year?"

"You mean 'Mr. Black, But Not Too Black'? Yes. That's what your father called him."

"That's the one," Felice laughed. "Dad sure had that dork pegged. You know what he had the nerve to tell me? He said that I read too many books and that I should start wearing make-up to make myself look lighter!"

"Oh my God! One of 'those.' I didn't think they still existed. Why was he dating someone as dark as you are anyway?"

"I think he wanted to prove that he was 'down.'" She raised her fist in a mock Black Power salute and they both laughed.

"Eventually, he gave up," Felice continued. "I still see him around. He's got a white girlfriend now."

"Well, at least he's being true to what he wants." Vetra paused. "You haven't had many phone calls from boys since then," she ventured.

"No. I've talked to a few, but none of them have seemed to like me," she said cagily.

"Oh come now, honey. You're a beautiful, smart young lady. Surely some of those little knot-heads at that school have recognized that."

"I just don't seem...to be what they want; most of them, anyway."

"You mean the black ones."

Felice looked up at her mother. "Yes."

"Felice, I know exactly how you feel. When I was your age, I went through exactly what you're going through now."

"You did?"

"Yes. Your father doesn't know this, but I had a white boyfriend before I met him."

Felice's mouth dropped open. "You're not serious. You never told Dad?"

"Think about how your father feels about white men. Do you think it's a good idea?"

"No!"

Vetra laughed. "A lot of the black men then thought that black women should walk two steps behind them, literally and figuratively--especially the ones who were caught up in 'Black Power.' It was so crazy! Supposedly they were trying to throw off the white man's shackles, but at the same time, they were trying to put shackles *on* black women. You know I wasn't having any of that!"

"Did you and your boyfriend ever...?

"What? Girl, no! You know your father was the first."

"Actually, no I didn't."

"Felice!"

"Well..." Felice began complacently.

"Wait a minute. I guess I shouldn't get so upset about your question. Your father was my first. But that's only because, right or wrong, that's the way a young lady behaved back then. Whenever you young ones hear about the sixties and the seventies, all you hear about is this 'free love' or 'changing mores' nonsense. Well it's a lot of hogwash, at least in my experience. Had I done any type of 'experimenting,' I would have been branded as 'loose' or 'easy' and no decent guy would have had anything to do with me; not like now."

Felice said nothing.

"Honey, you know, unlike your father, I try to stay out of your personal business, but right now, I'd like to ask you something personal."

"Okay."

"Are you...a virgin?" Vetra tensed a bit. In spite of her earlier thoughts, she wasn't sure if she wanted the answer to be 'yes' or 'no.'

"No."

"That's...fine. That's okay with me and that's as personal as I'm going to get. Wait, except for one thing: you were careful, weren't you?"

"Yes...he..." *they* "wore a condom. Can we talk about something else?"

Vetra ignored her request and pressed on. "Earlier I was thinking about myself at your age. If I had been born twenty-four years later, I might have...experimented a bit before I settled on your father. It sure would have made things easier on our wedding night."

"Mom!" exclaimed Felice. Like most people, her parents having sex was not a picture she liked having in her head. "Too much information!"

"Sorry, but you brought it up. It's just that, while I'm

happy with your father and would never dream of anyone else..."

Felice's eyes widened. "Mom?"

"Felice, stop it! You're eighteen years old. Well past old enough for me to speak with you plainly about sex."

"So, how come you never did this before now?"

"Fear...plain and simple, kiddo. I didn't know what to say or how to say it. Your grandma sure didn't have any kind of talk like this with me, except to inform me that a young lady kept her dress down and her legs closed."

Felice giggled. "Not exactly the advice we got in my sex ed class in high school."

"I would guess not. However, I should never have left sex education strictly up to that wonderful public school system in L.A. I guess I'm trying to make amends for it now. Is Kevin the one that you..."

Felice rolled her eyes. "No, Mom! I thought you said you weren't going to get any more personal."

"Oops! I forgot. Well I just want to say this: you already know more than I knew at your age and I'm happy, too, that you know to be physically careful. But what I'm worried about is your heart. Don't let anyone into it unless you know, or are pretty sure how they're going to treat it.

Some people take kindness as weakness and will walk over you just as easily as they take in air. Some men can be that way when it comes to sex. Not all of them, but some of them. I may not know too much about sex--or rather I only know about it with your father--but I have eyes. People like to say that things have changed for women; that they're free to do and be what they want. However, from where I sit, things haven't changed all that much."

Mom, you have no idea how right you are.

"So, Mom. What about your white boyfriend? Why did you guys break up?"

"Neither one of us could handle the pressure. I guess I should actually say, that neither one of us loved each other enough to handle the pressure. Your grandma and grandpa were cordial to him but they didn't want us together, and his parents were...well, you can guess. And the black men were ready to kill both of us. It would be different now. Every time I turn around, I see an interracial couple and it's great. And your grandma has since admitted that she was wrong."

"I sort of wonder if you're right about that, I mean about things being different."

"Why?"

"Last year, I remember a girl at school, who's since

graduated. She was a black girl and was real pretty, and all the black guys were like, 'Carrie' this and 'Carrie' that. They all were chasing her. Then she started to date this white guy and you should have heard the things they said about her."

"Don't tell me. Let me guess. White-boy lover; Race-traitor..."

"...and much worse. Never mind that nearly every black male athlete there has a girlfriend who is white or Latina."

"I guess things haven't changed as much as I had hoped."

"You know how it seems to me, Mom. It seems as though black men have gone and turned the tables on white men. I remember reading about the days when a white man could take any black woman he wanted, but woe to the black man who did the same. Now, it seems as though it's in the reverse."

"Not quite, honey. I have yet to hear of any white man who has been lynched for whistling at a black woman," said Vetra gently.

"Well yeah, you're right." Felice paused. "So, does that make what happened to you or Carrie right?"

"Of course it doesn't, dear. However, not being right

doesn't stop a whole lot of people from doing the things they do."

"That's for sure." Felice thought of Vonetta.

"If you and...Kevin start going out regularly, there's bound to be a lot of pressure on the both of you. Not just from black people, but from the white ones as well. If he's a football star, he's bound to be real popular with the white girls."

Felice then told her mother what had happened both times in the Quad with Mandy.

"That's exactly what I'm talking about. Make no mistake about it, there's nothing more vicious than a woman who's been tossed aside for someone else, especially if she deems that someone else to be 'beneath' her in some respect. And believe me, underneath, almost every white woman believes that she is more beautiful than the most beautiful black woman that ever lived. That one will not take losing to you lying down."

"So, you met Daddy right after you broke up with this guy?"

"Yes, about a month later. Your dad was different-- funny, but thoughtful, and not afraid of a strong woman. In fact, he seemed to like it when I displayed my brains or my strength-still does."

"Well, Dad does have three older sisters; all strong and all smart." One of Joseph's sisters was a doctor and the other two were college professors.

"And not about to hide the fact that they know everything."

Felice rolled her eyes. Her mother didn't always get along with her aunts.

"I think you should go out with this Kevin Hart," Vetra continued. If he likes you as much as you say, it's worth taking a little heat."

"Even from Dad?"

"You let me deal with your dad. Tomorrow's Friday, so he and I will have all day to discuss it before you talk to him."

"Going to soften him up for me first?"

"Of course, dear. What else is new?"

They both then heard the front door opening.

"Okay, Mom. I guess it's time for me to get out of here," she grinned.

"You better believe it!" She reached over to hug and kiss her daughter. "Do you know how much I love you and how proud of you I am?"

Warmed by her mother's embrace, she hugged her back.

"I love you, too, Mom."

The next day, Vetra and Joseph had the house to themselves, with both of their children at school. Felice, as every morning, left the house at around six-thirty, and Joey rode with Marta Garcia, mother of Pete. She and Vetra alternated carpool duties each day, and she had picked up the boy at seven. Vetra had gotten up to make sure that her children had a decent breakfast, but after they were gone, she climbed back in bed with her husband.

Every other day was filled with work, children, family, or church, but Vetra and Joseph had designated Fridays as their "us" day. Sometimes they would go for a walk in the near-by park, holding hands, giggling and whispering in the other's ear like teenagers. Other times, they would hash out arguments that they had let lie during the previous week.

On this particular Friday, Vetra and Joseph were lying snuggled up in their bed, lightly dozing. Friday was also love making day for them. Vetra had originally thought that setting aside a special day for making love would take all the fun and spontaneity out their sex life, but it had been necessary. Both of them were nearly always too tired for it on any other day. As it turned out, her fears were unfounded. The word "Friday" now had become a special, personal code between them. Whenever anyone else mentioned the day for whatever reason, both of them found themselves looking at each other knowingly and suppressing grins.

Vetra re-awakened easily. A tiny ray of sunshine, peaking between the drawn curtains, shone directly on her face. Not wanting to wake Joseph, whose arms and legs were wrapped around her, she was still. If only they could lie there contentedly in their bedroom basking in each others' warmth and love forever. She thought of the early days of their marriage, the years before Felice had been born. Joseph had recently graduated from college and Vetra was still in school. They had lived in a tiny apartment in L.A., barely bigger than the living room of their present house. Joseph had found a job as a manager in a grocery store and she had had a part time job. They had barely made enough money to pay their bills and keep food on the table, but those had been some of the happiest times of their lives. She and Joseph would lie in bed late into the night, sometimes making love and sometimes not. Always they would talk about their dreams and making plans for their future. They would wait a few years before having children so they could have a little time to get to know each other and to make a little money. Joseph had wanted a lot of children, but Vetra, an only child, wasn't sure that she wanted any at all and had told him so.

Vetra now laughed lightly at herself. How could she have been so stupid? Felice and Joey were the joys of both of their lives. Neither of them had given their parents much trouble, not like the children of so many of her friends in L.A.-no drugs or alcohol and no gangs or pregnancies.

She smiled as she remembered Joseph's face upon seeing his daughter for the first time. Her husband had always been a happy, exuberant man, but on that day eighteen years ago, as she watched him lift that small, brown, wriggling human for the first time, she had seen a joy never even considered alight in her husband's face. From that point on, she knew that Felice would forever be 'Daddy's Little Girl.'

When Felice was a little girl, Joseph had done everything with her. He had taken her to every museum, fair and amusement park in L.A. countless times. He had read to her each night and not just the standard fairy tales.

Occasionally, he would read a science fiction or mystery novel to her, the ones that had been written with teenagers in mind. As a consequence, Felice had already known how to read by the time she entered kindergarten.

The three of them would go camping and fishing at Lake Isabella each summer. Joseph would always bait Vetra's hook, since she refused to touch a worm. However, Felice would fearlessly bait the hook on her own small rod, while her mother watched with loathing and admiration, as the bait curled around her little girl's fingers.

Joseph had also bought Felice a small telescope. Though they hadn't been able to see much in the skies over L.A., Felice had been fascinated by the stars and had later poured over the encyclopedia in their home and memorized each planet in the solar system. She had been seven years old.

Joseph, who had been to several places in the world while in the army, also made sure that his daughter had a decent knowledge of geography. He had bought her a globe and a jigsaw puzzle of the United States. She had loved the puzzle and would take it apart and piece it together over and over again. The two of them had made a game of knowing what the capital of each state was and after a few months, they had changed the game to capitals of countries. Years later, in the year of the German reunification, Felice had wondered aloud why so many people she knew had no clue where Germany was; much less that it had been two countries.

"It's not that other people are stupid, Felice," her mother had replied. "It's just that most kids don't have a father like yours who took time out to teach you these things."

Yes, Joseph had been a wonderful father (and husband), but now, he was probably about to face his biggest challenge.

Remembering the conversation she had with her daughter the previous night, Vetra sighed lightly. "Daddy's Little Girl" was not so little any more, and she knew that Joseph was having a hard time with this. She once had to restrain him as they both had watched a man eyeing their daughter up and down with interest.

Men, thought Vetra now with amusement. The worse they are as young men, the harder they are on their daughters.

Joseph had told her about his single days; his early college years at NMU and his life in the army. He had been a typical jock at NMU, he had told her, catching any 'piece of trim' that had been thrown his way and not concentrating hard enough on the important things.

"You were fortunate not to have caught anything else," she had grinned at him. Sure enough, his grades dropped even below the already low standard of eligibility to play collegiate sports. He decided he'd had enough of school and had enlisted in the army. There, he had been a Morse Code Operator and had been fortunate enough to stay out of Vietnam during his one hitch, and he had continued to practice his tom-catting ways.

At the end of his enlistment, he decided to move to L.A. and to go back to school. He had enrolled in a community college, graduated, and transferred to Cal State Los Angeles, where he had met and immediately fallen in love with a slender, brown-skinned coed named Vetra Delaney.

And the rest is history, she thought as she felt her husband snuggle against her neck.

"Good morning," he said groggily. "Again."

"Good morning, yourself." She turned to give him a hug.

"What time is it?"

"Time for us to get out this bed and go do something fun."

Joseph stretched his sometimes stiff spinal column. "I think this old man has had his fun quotient for the week," he grinned at her.

"Come on, Old Man." She climbed out of the bed and put on her robe. "Let's get out into the real world."

The park was nearly empty, with it being mid-morning on a weekday. The slight frost, that had developed over night, was now nearly gone. The couple, hand-in-hand as usual, wore heavy coats and gloves, but where Vetra wore a purple knit cap over her thick hair, Joseph was hatless.

"I'm going to get you a hat in about a month for next winter. They should be on sale by then."

"Oh, so you're not going to get me one for my birthday, eh?"

"What I'm going to get you for your birthday is none of your business," she smiled at him.

"I'll really need it by next season to cover up some of this gray."

"I like the gray," she said as she reached up to touch his short sideburns.

"Yeah, sure."

"Well, I do. It's kind of sexy."

"Kind of like this little pouch I'm developing." He patted his incipient pot belly.

"Oh come on now honey! It's not nearly that bad. Besides, it gives me a little something to hold on to," she laughed as she grabbed a section of his middle.

"What's the matter, baby?" she asked. "Are you feeling a little old with your birthday coming up?"

"Maybe. Forty-five! How did that happen?"

"You know that I know how you feel. I can't believe that I'm forty.

"We're two old fogies for sure," he grinned. "I look in the mirror sometimes and get a shock when I see my father looking back at me."

"The same thing happens to me sometimes. I look at it and say, "hi Mom.'"

"That's okay, though. Anna's still pretty fine looking. I almost threw you over for her when I first met her," he teased.

She pinched him as he laughingly tried to get away.

"Most of the time I feel pretty good," he went on. "But sometimes when I look at Felice, I can almost feel another gray popping out of my head."

Vetra smiled. "Yes, I've been watching her, too. She's an adult now, Joe."

"Barely. In many ways she's still a little girl. Experience-wise, that is. We've kept her pretty sheltered. She has no idea what kind of snakes there are out there, just lying in wait to take a bite out of her."

"She and I had a long talk last night before you got home. She is not as naive as we'd like to believe. She's strong, smart, and independent, the way you raised her to be."

"We raised her to be that way."

"You are mostly responsible for all the good things our daughter is, honey." Here was the opening she had been looking for.

"Felice has a date tomorrow night."

"Is that right?" Joseph's face stretched into a predatory smile. "I guess I'll have to come home early tomorrow, to give the victim, uh, guy, the once over. Did she tell you his name?"

"Yes. It's Kevin Hart."

"What?!" Joseph's eyes widened, then he turned to look at his wife.

"You heard me."

"*The* Kevin Hart?"

Vetra sighed complacently in anticipation of the blowup. "Yes, honey, of the university's football team. The very same.

"A white man? She is not going anywhere with him! I forbid it! No daughter of mine is going anywhere with any white man! Not while I'm alive!"

"And how are you going to stop her? Are you going to lock her in her room and take away the car keys? What about school? They must see each other all the time there. Are you going to hire an armed bodyguard or get a restraining order to keep him away from her?"

"No! None of those things. But I am her father. She has to do what I say!"

"Does she? Remember that Felice is eighteen now. If she wanted to, she could move as far away from us as possible and there's not a thing we could do about it!"

"Are you saying that she threatened to move out if we won't let her go out with that...?"

"No, Joseph, I'm *not* saying that. Nothing of the kind came up. My point is that Felice is enough of an adult to be allowed to make some of her own decisions. Let's sit down on that bench over there and stop making a spectacle of ourselves." They sat.

"I remember what you told Felice about white men," she continued, "and how it would embarrass *you* to have one come to *your* house to pick up *your* daughter, as if everything were all about you. That's a pretty poor excuse, if you ask me. How in the world would something like that reflect on you, and even if it actually does, who the hell cares? It's not as though it's taking money out of our pockets or anything."

Joseph turned to look at her. "Vetra, if a white man comes to my house to pick up my daughter, it says that I've failed as a father."

"What? I'm sorry, honey, but I honestly do not get that one. What would that have to do with your fathering abilities?"

"To me, it's a rejection of black men...all of us...especially the one black man that's supposed to have the greatest impact on a young black girl's life: her father."

Vetra looked at him, comprehension dawning. "Ohh, I see now. Since many people unconsciously pick mates who are similar to their opposite sex parent, you would view a white mate for your daughter as a repudiation of *you*."

"That's it exactly."

"Do I look anything like your mother?"

"No, but..."

"So, your decision to marry a dark-skinned woman was a repudiation of your mother, right?"

"Of course it wasn't! It's not about appearance, I just happen to love you."

"Isn't it about appearance? Hasn't it always been about appearance? Not just between us, but between men and women or between light-skinned black folks and dark ones, or between black and white folks? Wasn't it appearance that caused your mother to take an instant dislike to me, just because I'm dark? Honey, it's *all* about appearance-always was and always will be."

"Vetra, racism may have started just because of appearance, but I don't have to tell you that it's blossomed into a whole different animal. It's a part of all of us who are descendants of slaves. We all have a little part of us that's been passed down from those times, a tiny little part that tells us that they are smarter, more beautiful and better than us; that we're not fit to be anything but the master's workhorse or mule or concubine. When I think of my daughter with a white man, I feel as though she would be telling the whole world that it's true that we're inferior; that's she's with a white man because she wants her children to be better, smarter, and more beautiful, and not to be like her old black father."

"I had a white boyfriend."

"You'd feel the same way probably if Joey..." Joseph stopped as his mind began to comprehend Vetra's words. "What...did you say?"

"Before you, I had a white boyfriend."

He was momentarily motionless, as if someone had cast a spell on him.

"You..." Joseph was again moving. He slowly turned to his wife, looking at her as though she were a stranger. *"You had a white boyfriend and didn't tell me?"* Joseph's voice was barely above a whisper.

"You would have..."

"You kept this from me for all this time...for twenty-one years? You married me, had my children and *you hid this from me?"*

"If I had told you, we would have never gotten married and never had our children! You had made it clear how you felt about white men. I loved you and didn't want to lose you. I still feel the same way. Joseph..."

He looked at her for a few seconds, part of him knowing that this was his lifetime mate. However, another part of him told him that he was looking at a stranger. He turned away from her.

Vetra tried to put her hand on his shoulder, but he flinched away from her.

"Joseph. You know that I love you. I made love to you, not him. I married you, not him. I had your children, not his."

He turned to look at her, the anger dying out of his face, being replaced by sadness, like a child who just found out that there was no Santa Claus.

"I'm going...home," he said tiredly. He got up off the bench at left her sitting there.

She sat watching his broad back, as tears began to stream down her face.

By the time Vetra reached the house, her face was dry. She opened the unlocked front door, came in and gently shut it.

"Joseph?" She cocked her head to see if her ears would give her a clue as to what part of the house he might be in. The bedroom-she could hear him rooting around in it, making the type of noise that she was unaccustomed to.

She headed towards the room expecting the worst and not hoping for the best. She knew that she had shaken the foundation of their marriage. But the truth was the truth. There was no point where she thought she should have told him earlier. Vetra wasn't the type of person to have regrets.

She half expected him to be packing his things, but when she entered the room, she found him sitting on the bed with one of their legion photo albums.

"Joseph?" He appeared not to have heard her. He was slowly turning each page, tracing his fingers over some of the images, laughing lightly or smiling at others.

"Joseph." He looked up at her with the sadness still etched on his face, but he beckoned to her.

"Come sit down and look at this," he said softly. With some trepidation, she did as he asked.

"Look at our children. Aren't they the most beautiful things you've ever seen?"

"Yes." She smiled at him uncertainly. "I always felt a little guilty thinking that way. Believing that one's own children are the smartest and best-looking children that ever lived is a way of inviting disaster, but I still think it anyway."

Joseph said nothing and turned his attention back to

the album. He turned the page and there was a photograph of his children taken eight years earlier. Felice's innocent, ten-year-old smile looked back at him. On her knee, she held a chubby Joey, who was grinning a baby's grin.

"Look at that, Vetra," he said softly. "Look at that picture. I remember thinking back then that those two perfect children were the sum of all the love and trust that existed between you and me, and that they were the living embodiment of what we had together." He closed the album and looked directly at her. "Today, I found out that what we had was a lie."

"I didn't lie to you Joseph."

"Not technically, no. But, you kept something from me that I needed to know. Omission is still a lie."

Vetra's fear was starting to turn into anger. "And why, may I ask, did you need to know this? It's not like I slept with the man." Joseph cringed as if an image in his own head were too much to bear.

"And even if I buy your answer," she continued with an intensity in her voice growing. "Even if I agree that I should have told you this before we got married, what do you think you would have done with this information?"

"I don't know," he lied.

"That's a crock! You know exactly what you would have done. You would have dropped me like a hot potato. You have long made it plain to me how you feel about white men. We've had disagreements about it for years..."

"And now I know why."

"No, you *don't* know why," Vetra snapped. "The reason why is that racism is wrong in whatever form it takes and from whoever it's coming, Joseph, whether it's from some Klansman or from you."

"So, you're going to compare me to a Klansman now?"

"You know I didn't mean it that way. Stop twisting what I say!"

"After all the things they've done to our people, and to our families, and to you and me personally, you're going to sit here and defend them to me?"

"Not *them*, Joseph, but the individual. You've always told me that you wanted to be taken for who you are, rather than what you are, and of course, that makes perfect sense, but, you have to do the same. Take each person for what he or she is."

"So, you expect all of us just to forget all of the things that have happened for the last four hundred years and are still happening, just like that! Vetra, that's against human nature and plain wrong."

"I'm not saying forget. I'm saying 'move on.' You know as well as I do that anger eats away at any person. Our anger, I mean our people's anger, has held us back for too long, in my opinion."

"So, we should turn the other cheek, eh," he sneered, "and end up with a bullet in it like so many others have? No, not this black man!"

"It's got to end somewhere, Joe, either with all of us dead, or with one of us refusing to perpetuate the cycle. Otherwise, we continue to go around in circles."

Joseph looked at his wife thoughtfully. "I understand that you feel this way and think that you might even be right. But I'm having trouble with it. And the actual issue remains this: you lied to me."

Vetra could think of nothing more to say. She watched with growing alarm as Joseph got up from the bed. He pulled open several of the drawers on his side of the chest. She watched mutely and helplessly as he opened the closet door to remove a shirt, a pair of jeans, and a small over-night bag.

"Where will you be?" she asked numbly.

"Over at Richard's." Richard was his brother.

"Fine."

She sat there on the bed, barely hearing him close the door. As she listened to the front door close, she idly wondered what she would do without him.

Chapter Six

"Mom?" Something was different. Usually when Felice came home from school, the smell of dinner would entice her before she even came in the door, whether it was food from the restaurant, or Vetra's own cooking. On Friday, her mother always cooked, since she had all day to prepare. However, on this day, there was nothing; no fish frying-nothing.

"Mom, are you here?" Some of the lights in the house were on, ones that wouldn't be on if no one was at home. Her parents were sticklers about saving energy; constantly berating her and Joey about leaving on unneeded lights. She walked into the empty kitchen and shut off the light.

"In here, Felice, in the bedroom," she heard her mother's tired-sounding voice call.

She walked in to see her mother sitting on the edge of the bed. Vetra still had on the clothes from earlier that morning, even the purple knit cap. Felice sat down next to her.

"Mom, what's wrong? Where's Daddy?"

"He's at your Uncle Richard's. I think he'll be there for the night...at least."

Fear stabbed through Felice's body. "What? What happened?"

"I told him about my old boyfriend."

"Oh no!" Felice put her head in her hands. "It's all my fault, Mom. All mine." She began to cry. "I'm so selfish! I'm sorry, Mommy."

Vetra was alarmed. She put her arms around her daughter.

"No! It definitely is not your fault, honey. It's mine. Mine for not telling your father the truth at the outset. Please don't cry, baby, please." She pulled Felice's head down on her shoulder.

"But, if I hadn't just had to have my way," Felice sobbed, "it would have never come up."

Vetra gently took Felice's face in both hands. "Yes, it would have. It would have--maybe not now, but sooner or later. The truth always comes to light, usually when you don't want it to. Here." Vetra grabbed a tissue from her vanity. "Come on, dry your eyes honey, and listen.

"It was my responsibility to be totally honest with the man I married, especially about something that I knew would mean something to him. *That's* why he's so angry with me, not because the guy was white. Your upcoming date with Kevin Hart was merely the catalyst for the truth to come out. It was God's way of telling me that it was time."

"But, you remember that you told me that it wasn't such a good idea for you to tell Dad about your boyfriend."

"Yes I do and you know what? I realized that I was teaching you the wrong lesson and putting you in a most difficult position. You should never have to choose between me and your father. Never.

"As for your lesson, it should be obvious." Vetra held her by the shoulders. "Trust the people that you care about. Trust them enough to tell them the truth. Sometimes it hurts, but it hurts more when you hold back for too long a time, say twenty or so years. Don't make the same mistake I have."

Felice looked at her mother, thinking of Laura Anderson, and of Kevin, and the Taus, and Daniel.

"What time is it?" Vetra looked around at the clock on the nightstand. "Oh my God, it's nearly five! Joey will be home soon and there's no dinner in the near future."

"How about I go get us some Chinese take-out?"

"Good plan."

"What are you going to tell Joey about Dad?"

"I'll tell him that Dad is over at Richard's and staying overnight and that's it. He'll think it's a sleep-over like he and Pete do."

"What if he asks you when Dad will be home?"

"I'll tell him the truth...that I don't know."

* * *

The next night, Felice was in a frenzy getting ready for her date. She'd had so few in her life that she had trouble knowing what to wear. Makeup was no problem; a little lotion and lip-gloss was all she ever wore. Maybe she would borrow her mother's brown lipstick.

She opened her closet with a sigh. Clothes however, were a different story. She couldn't remember the last time she had worn a dress, high heels, or panty hose. Her standard uniform in the winter was jeans, short boots, and a sweater. In the summer, it was jeans, sandals, and a tee-shirt.

There were a couple of dresses in the closet, bought by her mother, in the hopes that she would accompany them to Mass on a Sunday. When she had been sixteen, her parents had given her the option of not attending church if she didn't want to. She hadn't been back since.

Felice looked at one of the dresses with a grimace. It had been bought without her input, and though it was Felice's size, it looked more suitable for a large thirteen-year-old and she wouldn't go near it. Felice had chosen the second one herself. Her mother had dragged her, kicking and screaming, to the mall and forced her to pick one out. It was a simple, dark rust-colored dress with short sleeves. Felice pulled it out and held it against her in front of her full-length mirror. It was a couple of inches above the knees, but not too far. Great. Her dad would probably want her to wear a full shroud, covering everything but her eyes, like the Muslim women do, but her dad wasn't here.

She sat on her bed, the magnitude of that thought hitting her full force. When was Daddy coming home? She had wanted to cancel the date and go to her father to plead her mother's case, but Vetra wouldn't hear of it. She had practically ordered Felice to go out tonight.

"If you like Kevin and you want to go out with him, you're going to," her mom had said vehemently. "I don't care what your father says."

"But, Mom, if I don't go out with him, maybe this thing with you and Dad can somehow blow over," Felice had said desperately.

Vetra sighed. "You still don't understand, do you? What happened between me and your father wasn't about race mostly, it was about honesty, and it's something that will still be between us whether you and Kevin go out or not.

"And as for his feelings about white men, especially in relation to you, those are *his* feelings and that is *his* problem, not yours or even mine. This thing is something that he has to work out for himself. In the meantime, I refuse to let him give you the racism that our generation has had passed down to us. I refuse to let you be hurt by it in your own house. There's going to be enough of it out in the real world as it is."

"Okay, Mom, I understand. But how can I even have a good time knowing that you're here feeling sad about Dad and knowing that I'm part of the reason for it?"

"Girl, aren't you listening? You're not responsible for..."

"Yes, I am. This never would have happened if I hadn't given Kevin my phone number. You know it's the truth. Cause and effect-that stuff you guys have been preaching to me." Felice had said this last, with an ironic grin.

"So, does this mean you're going to judge who you like and associate with by how it's going to effect you parents' marriage? You know we didn't raise you that way. In spite of whatever your father and I are, you still have to be *you*, have to have your own likes and dislikes. Oh sure, we've tried to influence them. That's our job. But ultimately, you make your own decisions about your life. If you've heard anything we've been 'preaching' to you over these many years, I hope you heard that in there somewhere. Oh and, by the way, it's nice to know that you actually heard some of the 'sermons' we've given you. Judging by the look on your face sometimes, I wasn't quite sure that you did."

Felice had giggled. "You mean this look?" Felice feigned a bored look, her mouth dropping slightly open and her eyes glazing over into opaqueness.

"That's the one. I half expected you to roll your eyes a couple of times. If you had, I would have slapped you silly," her mother had said jokingly.

"I'll remember that." Felice had then grown serious again. "Dad has always told me the same thing about making my own decisions. But sometimes it seems that he doesn't really believe what he's telling me."

"He does. It's just that it's hard for him. It's hard for him to realize that his sweet little girl isn't a little girl anymore. Now when you make certain decisions, one's that he doesn't like, he realizes that, unlike before, there's little that he can do about it. It scares him."

"Doesn't it scare you?"

"Yes it does, a little, but not in quite the same way. There's a gulf of perception between men and women and it's never as wide as it is between a father and his daughter. Your dad told me that your grandpa Jean used to tell him that a man hadn't really been a father until he had fathered a girl."

"Yeah, well, he would have known. But why is it so difficult for a guy to have a daughter? Why is the gulf so wide?"

"A father, a good one like yours anyway, wants to give his daughter the world and wants to protect her, like any woman that he loves, from all pain and suffering. He wants to slay dragons for her. Oh sure, your dad would slay a dragon or two for me, but he'd slay a whole army of them for you, kiddo.

"At the same time, he realizes that he can't protect his daughter from everything and everyone, so, if he's a good father, he tries to give his daughter the tools to protect herself.

"The biggest frustration for a father like yours, however, is this: even if he slays all of his daughter's dragons and gives her all the tools to slay a few of her own, there will always be one more out there. And sooner or later, neither he nor his daughter will be able to prevent that dragon from breathing fire on her. The daughter will have to take it like a woman.

"Then there's that gulf, his daughter *is* a woman, with all the connotations that a man carries in his head of being a woman. Even if a father and a daughter have the absolute best relationship in history, the father knows that there's a gap in their communication, simply because he's a man and she's a woman. There's a place in her life, a place that a girl's mother understands (hopefully), that he can never comprehend, simply because he's not a woman. Look at you and me. Until recently, you and I were like cats and dogs. Now, I find out you're more like me than I ever even imagined." Her mother smiled. "What a scary thought."

"I get this feeling sometimes that there are certain things that you 'get' that Dad doesn't," said Felice. "Not because he doesn't want to, but just because he doesn't understand."

"That's what I'm talking about exactly. Simply put, he has no idea, of course, what it's like to *be* a woman. So, when he watches what women go through and thinks of his daughter, he can't help but think of all of the other women that he's known; the good ones *and* the bad ones. He then starts to think of all the ways that a woman can be hurt by a man. After that, he starts to think of all the women that *he's* hurt and says to himself, 'not my daughter, no sir.' That's why most men look at any potential suitor of their daughter as the enemy.

"Figuratively speaking."

"Hopefully." Vetra paused. "Maybe it's better that he won't be here when Kevin picks you up tonight."

Now as Felice got ready, she thought that her mother had been wrong about that. She *wanted* her father there when Kevin came, even if he didn't behave (and she doubted that he would be totally rude). She had hidden so much of her life from her parents for so long, and she now wanted to stop hiding from the two people she loved most in the world, especially her father. If Kevin was going to be a part of her life, she didn't want to slink and hide it from Dad. She would fight her father over it, if need be, but she would be honest about it. No more secrets.

She thought about some of the girls she had gone to school with in L.A. Some had fathers who were in prison or were on drugs or were alcoholics or were dead. Some had mothers who had had so many men in and out of the house that they didn't even know who their father was. Some had abusive fathers or stepfathers or boyfriends of their mothers, who beat them and/or raped them. Then there was her own father, who kissed, loved, and hugged her in an absolutely fatherly way, who barely took a drink, who told her jokes, who had never spanked her, who had given her as much knowledge as he could conceive, and who always had time to listen to what she had to say. He could be strict, but he was never mean. Now, after her experience with the Taus, she understood his strictness, his protectiveness. He had tried to keep all the dragons away from her, but, as Mom had said, he couldn't slay all of them. Especially not the ones he didn't know about; the ones who Felice, herself, had let burn her.

Felice started as she heard the doorbell ring. She looked at herself in the bathroom mirror. *Pretty ugly.* In the last couple of years, she had grown pretty confident about her physical appearance after a seemingly endless period of teenaged gawkiness. In color-struck L.A., she had constantly been compared unfavorably against the lighter-skinned, fuller-figured black girls. And she had to admit, most of them were more attractive than she had been with her long, gangly, stick-like limbs and her ever-troublesome hair which had been broken off by too many harsh relaxers. Then, at sixteen, she had cut off her hair and stopped straightening it and at about the same time, her body had started to become, rounder and fuller, more womanly. She was still slender, but as she became more confident, she began to glide, rather than stomp on her long, narrow feet.

She had thought, like most women, that men preferred long hair, but as soon as she cut hers, suddenly she began to receive more and more compliments on her hair, mostly from her male schoolmates. No one had ever complimented her on her hair when she straightened it.

"Mom, would you get that, please?" she shouted.

"Of course, dear," she heard her mother chuckle.

So, as a result, she now usually thought of herself as pretty hot stuff--except in situations like this one. It seemed that every blotch on her face had picked this day to turn up. And was that a new zit she saw trying to pop up on her forehead? She touched it. *Great*, she thought as she felt the familiar soreness. *It's gonna look like Vesuvius in a day or two.*

She turned on the tap, ran her hands through it, and patted her hair. At least it was cooperating. He had seen her before, she finally decided with a shrug. If he threw up when he saw her, she'd know that she didn't look so hot. Just as she started to shut off the light and make her entrance, she halted. *Put some lotion on those hands you just wet, goofy.*

She could hear her mother's and Kevin's voices in the living room as she walked down the hall. She suppressed a giggle at her mother's bright 'getting-to-know-you' tone. They were lightly laughing at some small joke just as she entered the living room.

Kevin found himself feeling uncharacteristically nervous as he turned his father's two-year-old Volvo onto I-40. He had been out with many girls before and had met many parents before. Heck, he had been out with *this* girl before. But some part of him knew that Felice was more than just any girl. Some part of him felt happiness whenever he thought of her, some part of his heart leapt for joy whenever he saw her. Now, he was about to meet the very reasons for her being on the planet. For the first time in his life, he wondered whether he would measure up.

He considered the fact that he might be nervous because they were black, but then dismissed it. If Felice's parents didn't want her to date a white guy, surely she would have mentioned something about it. Surely, she would have warned him. She probably wouldn't have even agreed to go out with him. Wait a minute! Maybe that's why she had driven away almost without a word that day at the mall. Maybe that's why she seemed so reluctant to give him her phone number!

Boy, you're really slow sometimes, he thought as he reached up to thump himself in the head.

He got off the highway at the Lomas exit. What was he about to walk into? Would Felice's father put a shotgun in his face as soon as he walked into the door? Did he really want to put himself in that type of situation? He remembered that Felice's father had been born on the same day as his own father. If Mr. LeCroix and his father were anything alike, Mr. LeCroix would be totally civil with him, even laugh and joke with him. But, covertly, he would be watching him like a hawk, waiting for a weakness that he might be able to use. When he found that weakness, he would go for Kevin's jugular. Kevin shuddered at the memory of seeing his father do the same type of thing.

At last he found Las Palmas Southwest. What was that number? He looked at the strip of paper he had scribbled the address on. 1435.   There it was; a nice, medium-sized house typical of Albuquerque, modeled after the pueblos that Indians had created thousands of years ago. Was its peaceful appearance a cover? Should he park and go on in, or should he turn around and go home and save himself from having to look down the business end of a firearm?

If he did that, if he just turned around and went home, if he called Felice and made up some excuse, what would happen? He knew, didn't he? He'd never be able to look Felice in her beautiful face again. He'd never be able to look at himself in the mirror again.

He parked and got out, pulling his jacket from the back seat. He knew he looked good in his dark suit, especially made for his hard-to-fit frame. His hair had been freshly cut that afternoon and freshly moussed that evening. At least they couldn't say he looked like Charles Manson. But what if they thought he looked like Ted Bundy?

With that disturbing thought swirling in his head, he rang the doorbell. When the door opened, he found himself looking down into the smiling face of a shorter, slightly older-looking, very beautiful version of Felice.

"Uh, hello...I'm Kevin Hart."

"Hi, Kevin. I'm Vetra LeCroix, Felice's mother." She extended her hand. "Come on in, dear. Felice will be out in a minute."

He shook her hand. Then he stepped in and briefly looked around; a nice, warm, comfortable-looking living room and not a rifle case in sight. He turned back to her. "I'm sorry, Mrs. LeCroix. I was a little surprised when I came in. You look like Felice's sister, not her mother. But I remembered she told me that she only had a brother, so I was confused."

Vetra laughed. "First brownie points are successful. Let's sit down and see if you can make some more. And please, call me Vetra. Mrs. LeCroix is my mother-in-law. Come. Sit down."

"You don't still call your mother-in-law that, do you?" Kevin said as Vetra led him to a spacious couch.

"When I first met her, of course I called her 'Mrs. LeCroix.'" She sat down next to him. "For years, even when Felice was of a good size, she never asked me to call her anything else. Then, when I gave birth to my first and only boy-child, my son Joey, she asked me to call her 'Martine.' Go figure."

"You're kidding." Kevin was astounded.

"No, I'm not. My husband's mother is a traditionalist. To her, a woman isn't a real woman unless she's married and has given her husband a son."

Kevin had no idea how to respond. So he looked around. "Nice house," he said, meaning it. The decor was simple, with plants as the main motif. Real ones, not ones depicted in the upholstery. Even in winter, Vetra managed to keep everything green.

"The plants give the room a sense of...life," he continued. "Like they want to reach out and grab you."

"Don't say that within earshot of my son. That kid has just too vivid an imagination. He'll be waking up later tonight, saying, 'Mommy, the rhododendron's coming to get me!'"

It was during their laughter that Felice chose that moment to make her entrance.

"Well there she is," Vetra said with an approving smile. Kevin turned toward Felice and stood up, uncharacteristically speechless. She was the most beautiful thing that he'd ever seen.

"Hi...," he ventured.

"Hi, Kevin. You look nice, like one of those guys in a Calvin Klein ad."

"Um, thanks, I think...you look, you look..."

"I don't know, but I'm pretty sure that Kevin likes the way you look," said Vetra. "Too bad your dad's not here to see you."

"Is your husband still at work? Felice's told me a little bit about him. I was looking forward to meeting him."

"He'll probably work late tonight," Vetra said cryptically. "Maybe next time."

They all then turned toward the door as they heard the rattling of keys. Kevin, who was still standing, straightened his back and smoothed his suit. Who knew? He might have to be buried in it.

The lock gave way and in stepped a tall, handsome, broad-shouldered black man, nearly of a height with Kevin. His nearly-black eyes swept the room at lightening speed and came to rest momentarily on Kevin's blue ones.

Then, almost absently, the man stepped forward to kiss Vetra on the cheek. Then he turned to look at Felice. Felice looked back at the man. "Hi, Daddy," Kevin heard her say softly with just a touch of happiness, or so Kevin thought.

Kevin again looked into those dark eyes trying to see what was in them, to no avail. Then, suddenly, before Kevin knew what was happening, the man was right in front of him, offering him his hand.

"Hello, I'm Joseph LeCroix."

"Hello, sir. I'm Kevin Hart," said Kevin, suddenly wanting to be anywhere else, like, say, on offense on his own one-yard line.

Joseph had an iron grip, as Kevin expected. Kevin could smell the aromas of countless spicy foods wafting from Joseph's clothing, as Joseph inspected him.

"You were better last year."

"I'm sorry?"

"Last year...before you broke your leg."

"Oh. Yes, sir, I know," said Kevin complacently.

"You've lost a little bit of mobility. But you're young yet. You've got a lot more scrambling to do."

"Felice tells me that you played defense for the Tigers twenty-five years ago."

"Sure did. I flunked out though, and went in the army. It was for the best. I needed to do a little growing up. Besides, if I'd have stayed here, I never would have met Felice's mother. Have a seat," Joseph gestured to the couch and set himself in his easy chair.

"That would have definitely been a tragedy." Kevin said, glancing quickly at Felice. "My father went to NMU about the same time you did."

"Really? What's his name?"

"Herbert. He's a lawyer here."

"Yes, I've heard his name recently, but I don't recall anyone by that name in school. Was he a jock?"

"Not hardly," Kevin grinned. "He was in all the 'geek' clubs, like the Latin club and the Poli Sci club..." Kevin suddenly felt Felice's eyes on the back of his head.

"Then I definitely didn't know him," grinned Joseph. "I didn't exactly have education on my mind when I was there. I played football, partied, and chased girls. This was way before I met Mrs. LeCroix of course. I gather that you don't belong to any of the type of clubs that your father belonged to."

"No, sir."

"Just into playing football, right?"

"Yes, sir."

"And having a good time, too, right?" Joseph smiled benignly. He stood up and walked over the mantle of the fireplace.

"Well...sometimes, sir."

"Just make sure you don't have too good of a time with my daughter," Joseph said evenly. Those dark eyes shone with just the slightest hint of menace. His smile was gone.

"Oh, no sir," Kevin said shakily, feeling as though his jugular had been punctured. As he stood up, he yelped as he slammed one of his knees into the coffee table. He looked to see that Joseph was suppressing a laugh. He turned around to look at Felice, but she and Vetra had retired to the kitchen. He thought he could hear their identical-sounding laughter.

"No need to put yourself on the injured list," said Joseph, still trying to keep a straight face. The menace had lessened somewhat, but was still there. "Just treat my daughter with respect and you have no need to worry about me."

"Of course, sir. I never considered treating her otherwise," said Kevin, resisting the urge to rub his left knee.

"Good." Joseph went to the kitchen door and stuck his head in.

"Well, are you going out with the man or aren't you?" Kevin heard him ask Felice. He couldn't quite make out what Felice said, but he did pick out the words 'scare' and 'shotgun.'

"No. He hasn't given me a reason to...yet," Joseph answered her, matter-of-factly.

In a few seconds, there was Felice. His heart was doing that unfamiliar flippy-flop thing again, only now it was no longer so unfamiliar. For her, he could brave her father's menace, maybe even his shotgun.

"Are you ready to go?" Kevin asked her.

"Sure." She retrieved her winter coat and scarf from the hook that stood near the front door.

"Here," he said as he took her coat from her and helped her put in on. He could see the LeCroixs out of the corner of his eye; Vetra with a slight smile, Joseph mostly expressionless except for the eyes, which narrowed like a cat. Kevin turned to face Vetra and Joseph.

"We'll be back at about eleven, if that time is okay with the two of you."

"That's fine," Vetra said. Kevin saw her grab her husband's arm. "Be sure to drive safely," she said cheerfully.

"Yes, ma'am, I will. Goodnight and nice to meet both of you."

"Goodnight and same to you, dear," said Vetra. Kevin looked at Joseph and saw that he had gotten all the pleasantries he was going to get from him on this night. Still, he nodded his head at the man and received a slight, almost imperceptible nod in return. Kevin felt grateful to have received that much.

He heard the door close as he and Felice headed down the path leading to the street. She looked up at him.

"That went pretty good," she grinned at him.

"Really? I was kind of waiting for your dad to run me out of there," he said as they began to walk down the street toward his father's car.

"If he didn't think you had honorable intentions, he would have."

"So, you think my intentions are honorable, eh?" he smiled at her. Then, suddenly, he felt the hair on the back of his neck stand up, as though his back were in the cross-hairs of some high-powered scope. He turned his head back toward Felice's house. At one of the windows, the light from the inside framed the darkness of a tall, broad-shouldered, unmoving human being, looking unmistakably in his direction.

* * *

As he watched the car drive away, Joseph was feeling another set of eyes boring into his own back. Reluctantly, he turned around to face his wife. The two stared at each other for what seemed to be a long while. Then Joseph wearily sat himself on the couch. Taking his cue, Vetra walked over to the easy chair and sat down.

"Thanks, Joe."

"For what?"

"For not coming in here brandishing a gun at the kid."

Joseph shrugged his shoulders. "What good would that have done? It would have made you and Felice mad at me for a long time and probably would have literally pushed her into his arms. But, don't think I didn't think about it."

She chuckled slightly. "I figured as much."

The two gave each other shy looks, as if they were courting again.

"We should get this out of the way before one of the kids gets home," he said to her evenly.

"Get what out of the way, Joseph?" Her voice was like steel. "I did what I thought was best. Not out of deceit, but out of love--the wrong thing for the right reasons."

"I know."

Vetra looked as if she had been punched. "You what?"

"I said I know. Looking at the whole thing reasonably, remembering how I was back then, I can't blame you for not telling me." He grinned at her puzzled look. "Didn't expect that did you?"

"You'd better believe I didn't." She paused and then took a heavy intake of breath. "So, how are things between us, I mean you and me?"

Joseph looked at the face that was more beautiful than when he'd first seen it long before. "I don't know, honey.

Intellectually, I understand your reasons for keeping what you kept from me, just like, intellectually I know that there's nothing wrong with Felice dating that kid."

"But emotionally…"

"Yes, my emotions are another story. It's almost as though there's a blockage in my throat every time either of the two subjects enter my mind. It's going to take some time before I can process this stuff."

"I guess I'll have to be content with that." She hesitated again. "Are you staying at Richard's again tonight?"

"No, Baby. My place is here."

Vetra smiled, got up from the chair and went over to sit next to him. "As it always will be," she said as she raised her hand to gently stroke his cheek.

* * *

"This Baklava is delicious. My dad makes something similar in the restaurant."

"I thought you said that your father's restaurant is Creole."

"It is, but my dad's picked up recipes and cooking techniques from all over. He's not so rigid when it comes to food."

"But, when it comes to a white guy dating his daughter...," Kevin started gingerly.

"You could tell, eh? I thought you seemed a little nervous."

"What do you mean, 'you thought?'" He said, grinning. "I could hear you and your mother laughing at me when I slammed my knee on your coffee table!"

Felice started laughing again. "Sorry," she said sheepishly. "We tried to get into the kitchen in time but it was too late."

"Your dad almost burst out laughing, too. I guess it was 'laugh at the goofy white boy' night."

"Hey, it could have been worse. You could have done a Chevy Chase and flipped *over* the table."

He laughed. "True. That would have done wonders for my football career."

"Not to mention your neck." Suddenly she grew serious. "Are you worried about my dad?"

"I'm not sure yet. Does this mean that you'll go out with me again?"

She smiled shyly at him. "Maybe."

"Then, yes, I'm worried about your dad."

"Please don't be. He's a smart, reasonable guy, most of the time."

"Except when it comes to his little girl."

"I'm not a little girl."

"Don't I know it. But to him you are."

"What I'm trying to say is, that I think he'll come around once he gets used to the idea of us being...friends."

"Friends, eh?" He grinned as he leaned across the table closer to her. "Okay, I can accept that."

"Good because...," she broke off. The purposefully loud conversation from another table was wafting over to them. The restaurant was a bit crowded with it being Saturday night, so both Felice and Kevin knew that they were meant to hear it.

"What's a nice boy like that doing with *her?*" It was a woman's voice. Felice turned to look at her. She looked just like Mrs. Castle, her ninth grade teacher, who had been one of her favorites. Even the large gray eyes were the same shape. However, they didn't have in them what Mrs. Castle's eyes had contained. And this mouth was slightly twisted, as if the woman had eaten Joseph LeCroix's red-hot jambalaya.

"I don't know. Back in my day, we didn't take nigger gals out to dinner before we did our business with 'em.

Times are changing." Kevin looked over at the man. He was a dead ringer for his father--the same Herbert Hart who had taught him that about most of the countries in the world; who had taken him to India; who had taken him along to Washington D.C. to protest South African apartheid.

Kevin sprung up out of his chair like the lightning for which Malik had nicknamed him.

"Kevin, don't do it," he heard Felice's firm voice say. "They're stupid."

He appeared not to heed her words. He noted, with grim satisfaction, the fear on the faces of the couple, as they saw the large young man coming toward them. He then heard them gasp in relief as he passed them by to head toward the maitre'd station. He turned to wink at Felice, as he heard her laughter waft over to him.

* * *

Ten minutes later, as the loudly protesting couple was being escorted out by the restaurant security, Kevin sat down to face Felice again.

"I thought you were going to turn their table over," she said to him, grinning.

Kevin grinned evilly. "I think they did, too. I felt like it, but that wouldn't have gone over well with the owner, who's a friend of my dad's."

"And if *you* did something like that, it would be all over the papers, probably on the front page."

"Well, my motives were a little self-serving, yes. But, as my dad says, the clout is mightier than the sword."

Felice's face was unreadable. "I guess. You know if we...hang out together, this type of thing is bound to happen again. You can't have everyone 'thrown out.' Like on campus, for instance. There's bound to be someone who doesn't like us hanging together. Your friend, Mandy comes to mind."

"Mandy's not my mom, or my girl either. I'm free..."

"White..." she filled in.

"And 21," he finished sheepishly.

She laughed at his expression. "I guess it became an expression for a reason."

"Yep," he sighed. "Probably if you asked Malik, he'd tell you the entire history of the saying. He's a real pain in the... butt about that stuff."

Felice giggled. "You know it's not like I haven't heard the word 'ass' before. I might have used it a couple of times, too--in relation to donkeys, of course."

"No!" Kevin said with mock surprise. "My pristine image of you is ruined."

"Oh well. Seriously, there will be more incidents like that one. Maybe not so blatant, but we'll get some funny looks."

"I don't see why, especially on campus. I see lots of interracial couples there. As a matter of fact, I've hardly ever seen Malik with a black girl."

"That's probably because there aren't so many."

"There's quite a few that I've taken note of. Malik and I counted one day. Almost every black girl we saw was alone or with another girl, including you."

"I'm not terribly social," said Felice evenly.

"You seem pretty social to me," he smiled at her.

"Well, when a guy shushes his harem just to say 'hi,' you've just *got* to talk to him."

He reddened slightly. "That wasn't my harem. They're just my..."

"Groupies?"

"...friends."

"Oh."

"You sound a little jealous."

"Of them? I *don't* think so. Just curious is all. Must be a jock thing. Male jocks. My friend Adrienne doesn't have a horde of guys following after her."

"Adrienne Anderson?

"Yes."

"I know who she is; the star of the women's round-ball team. That's your friend?

"My best friend."

"Hmm. Too cool. As for no men following after female athletes, it's because no one thinks that a female athlete is going to be rich when she graduates."

"True." She paused for a moment. "So you plan on being rich when you graduate, eh?"

"If my dad can swing it. He's going to go full time as my agent when I get to the NFL."

"Sounds cozy. Do you love anything besides playing football?

He looked at her intensely. Rarely had any girl ever asked him that question. "Yes. Yes I do. I love animals: Dogs, cats, fish, and horses. We've got the first three at my house and my uncle has a ranch in south Texas that we go to every year to ride. I like a lot of other animals, too."

"You think you'd be a vet, if you weren't playing football?"

"I had thought about it, yeah. But, I also wouldn't mind being a lawyer like my dad."

"You can do that and play football, too, you know."

"Yeah, maybe."

"You don't sound too convinced."

"That's 'cause I'm not," he grinned. "I know myself. Once I get to the NFL, I don't think I'll have the discipline to concentrate on law school."

"Well, you know better than I do, but I bet if you put your mind to it, you'd make it."

He looked at her quizzically. "So what are you going to be when you grow up?"

"A lawyer, thanks for asking," she said sarcastically.

"That figures. You know how to make a good case. Wait 'til you meet my dad. Soon as he finds out that you want to be a lawyer, you will be able to do no wrong in his eyes."

They chattered on, with Kevin not even realizing what he had just said. He had never taken a girl to meet his father.

An hour later, as they pulled up in front of the LeCroix house, both of their minds were churning in anticipation, exhilaration, and fear. After they parked, Felice sat impatiently waiting for Kevin to come around and open her door.

"Mademoiselle,' he said, as he opened the door.

She smiled at him as she climbed out. Stretching to her full height, she was nearly as tall as he was due to her shoes. Her own nervousness was starting to subside as she saw that he was far more nervous than she. As she watched him apprehensively run his hand over his own hair, she gently tucked her arm under his.

"Would you be so kind as to escort me to my door, sir?"

"Sure thing, M'lady, if I don't fall over first." They laughed as they made their way up Felice's front walk.

Kevin felt his knees nearly give out on him as Felice tucked her long-fingered hand under his arm. He made

some small joke and, as they both laughed, the other part of
his brain said, *here it comes*!

Why was he so nervous? He'd kissed lots of girls
before. Granted, he had never kissed a black girl before, but
it appeared that they had two lips just like everyone else. He
turned to look at Felice's lips. The lip stick she had been
wearing had worn off and she hadn't bothered to replace it.
She didn't need to. Her lips were wide, brown, and smooth.
Next to her shining brown eyes, they were the most attractive
part of her face....

"Kevin?"

"Yes?" For some reason he hadn't noticed that they
had stopped at her front door.

"Dinner was really good."

"I'm glad you liked it. What did you think of the
company?"

"He was okay too," she teased.

"I guess I'll have to settle for that. See you on Monday
in the Quad around eleven?

"Eleven it is."

Kevin had in his mind to turn and make his way back
down the walk, when Felice took both of his hands in hers
and gently kissed him on the lips.

He was nearly frozen with surprise, however his lips responded.

"See ya later," she said after she pulled back, grinning at the stunned look on his face.

A slow smile spread across his face. "You bet you will."

Chapter Seven

Malik trudged on his long, powerful legs away from his last class for the day in a bad mood. Or, at least he was showing his bad mood to the outside world, which was unusual for him. As was so with Kevin, nearly everyone on campus greeted him as he passed, whether they knew him or not.

Normally, Malik was very humble about his small-town celebrity status and, unlike many of his teammates, made a conscientious effort not to appear to be an egomaniac, but not today. Instead of the sunny, warm "hello/hi there" that was his customary greeting to every living soul who passed him, all they got from him was a terse "hi" on this day. He was furious, and for a man who was very slow to anger, this was a scary situation.

Usually, Malik rolled with the punches and he had taken a lot of punches in his lifetime. Sometimes it seemed as though no one in his life would accept him for what he was; no one, but his father, that is, and sometimes his friend, Kevin.

A genius is what he was; a certified genius. He had been given the standard IQ test at age seven. Afterward, the authorities at his elementary school had wanted to skip him forward two grades, from second to fifth, but his late mother wouldn't allow it. A compromise was struck and Malik skipped only one grade.

"The boy is going to be enough of an outcast as it is," he had overheard Cynthia Hayes say to his father. "You know how our people are, Elijah. They are like crabs in a barrel. Let one try to climb out of the barrel, and they do everything they can to pull him back down. You should know quite well. It was done to you and your two other sons."

"So does that mean we should 'keep our place?' I've had enough of that crap, Cyn. I may not have been the perfect father to Randy and Alex, may not have been there when they needed me, and may not have encouraged them when they needed my encouragement, but I can at least try to do better by Malik. And, I won't be doing that if I teach him to hide the fact that he's smarter than damn near everybody, black, white, or indifferent."

That conversation had shaped everything that Malik was. From that day to this, he had struck a sort of compromise in his life, with the abetting of his father. He would show the standard face to the world at large, black or white; that of the entertainer. Privately, however, Malik Hayes made the most of his gifts.

For his part, right after the IQ test, Elijah Hayes had (unsuccessfully) submitted his seven-year-old son to be a member of MENSA, and both parents had supplemented their youngest child's education outside of the dismal public school system through libraries, museums, science fairs, and the like. Malik was Elijah's pride and hope: his last chance at bringing a functioning man-child into adulthood and Malik knew this. He would not let his father down.

Malik's parents were older than most of his peers' parents due to his being a late-in-life, unexpected child. Randall was his oldest brother, nearly old enough to be his father. Neighbors had occasionally reported seeing Randy, staggering out of an alley or coming out of a known dope house. Alexander, ten years Randall's junior, had chaffed under his father's restrictions and had moved out at age sixteen. He had been in and out of juvenile corrections, had been a known gang member, and had had no legal job that Malik had known about. When Malik was twelve, Alex had been killed, shot in the back of the head, by unknown assailants. Witnesses, however, had known who they were. But none in his/her right mind went to the police. (Cynthia Hayes' health, both emotional and physical, had been permanently impaired by the murder of her son and she had succumbed to a fatal stroke not many years afterward.)

Such varying influences had taught Malik to play his own special game. His superior intellect told him that if he wanted to be able to get along with his peers, he would have to find something that obscured the fact that he was a consistent honor student. He found two things: an innate sense of humor and sports.

His father had, at first, discouraged his involvement in sports: "you're not going to grow up to be another court jester or gladiator." But Elijah had relented under pressure from his wife. "The boy's gotta have some outlet for all that

stuff rolling around in his brain or he'll go crazy," she had
warned. When Elijah had seen how much his son had
enjoyed football and how good he was at it, he had sighed.
His other sons had been just as promising in that area.

So, Malik spent his young life playing at being the
homeboy and really being the scholar under cover. He had
grown to his adult height, six feet three inches, by the time
he was sixteen, and had his mother's caramel-colored skin,
and her sunny disposition (the one she'd had before Alex's
death). He had his father's straight back and his white,
even-toothed smile, and his own wicked sense of humor. As
a result, he was universally popular wherever he went. The
reputations of his brothers, and later, his own athletic
reputation, kept him from being hassled by the street gangs.
His athleticism also protected him against the syndrome that
so many intelligent black children suffer from in their
elementary and secondary school years: being stigmatized
for "wanting to be white."

Girls, of course, adored him and he liked them right
back. He'd had several dates with the prettiest and most
popular of his female classmates by the time he finished
high school and he wasn't a virgin, but, oddly enough, he
had never had a steady girlfriend. He had wondered at this,

but Elijah hadn't. He knew that if his son kept looking for female companionship among the cheerleaders and the homecoming queens of the world, Malik was unlikely to find a girl that he could stand talking to for more than a few minutes.

And on this day, Malik had learned that lesson yet again.

Unlike many black people, Malik was very conservative politically. He hated the concept of affirmative action. It made him feel as though white people were giving him a handout because he was genetically too stupid to earn a place in a college or at a job on his own. (Not many people knew that Malik was at New Mexico University on an academic scholarship rather than an athletic one.) He knew that his brothers and his sister were just as smart has he was, but hadn't succeeded in life because of their *own* choices, rather than being held back by some phantom white man. Nobody had forced Randall to become an addict. Nobody had forced Alex to become a gang-banger. And even though his sister, Regina, was respectably employed by the Army, Malik knew that she had so much more potential than she was probably using, as the enlisted woman that she was. Choices were the key to success, Malik believed. Oh, he had no illusions that there were still quite a few white racists out there. He had run into enough of them as a teenager in Detroit, and right here in the "Land of Enchantment," but he'd be damned if he'd let them have any power over him. He'd be damned if he let them be right in saying that blacks were inferior. He'd be damned if he let their "prophecy" come true: that he'd end up in jail, have a bunch of illegitimate babies by a bunch of women, be an addict, be a gang-banger, or be a drain on society. He wondered why so many of his peers didn't understand that when they made these types of choices, that they were playing right into the hands of the racists. In this year, his first being of age to vote in a presidential election, he planned to cast his vote for the incumbent; a Republican.

In his World History course, Malik was the star, as in nearly every other subject he had taken. In high school, he had been fascinated by the causes of World Wars One and Two and morbidly fascinated by the Third Reich. Additionally, he was fascinated by the Cold War--which appeared to be at an end--the Soviet Union, and had done as much reading as a graduate student on the subjects. He was riveted by the Warsaw Pact's disintegration right before his eyes.

However, his brilliant, but still teenaged mind, found it difficult to grasp how a people could set out to purposely and so efficiently wipe out another group of people. Hitler and Stalin had deliberately gassed, shot, and starved their own countrymen and those of other countries, simply to reduce the numbers of any who might oppose their efforts to gain and retain power. The two had brainwashed their people; set up a particular group as an "enemy," used seemingly plausible means to prove that a chosen group was the enemy, and then destroyed that group. It was brilliant, Malik had to admit--horrifying and disgusting, but brilliant. And their hoodwinked countrymen had just let it happen!

Malik had long ago vowed that he would visit Germany and Russia someday to find out if they were somehow different from the rest of humanity. Though his brother had been murdered, evil hadn't yet bared its face enough to him for his keen intellect to discern, identify, and study it. He was nineteen years old.

In spite of Malik's patently broad knowledge base, there were always those who thought that brains, athletic talent, and brown skin could not possibly come in the same package and one of them had picked this day to test him. He should have been beyond getting angry. It always happened eventually whenever he took a class any more mentally taxing than typing. Yet, each time, he could feel his face burn with the desire to put his knuckles into a smug, usually white, usually male face.

Oh they'd just love that. The nigger shows his true colors. We always knew he'd revert to type. They all do eventually.

But on this day, the face was that of a girl. And, this time, it was the only other black face in the class; that of a girl named Ayesha. Ayesha was one of the Tigers' cheerleaders. Malik knew her on a casual basis and they had talked a little bit, flirted, and laughed. But, he had stopped speaking to her because he had overheard a conversation of hers. She had said to another girl that Malik was a just another white girl-loving, race traitor, and that the only thing he could do for her was spend his money on her.

Ayesha was usually fairly quiet during a lecture, only occasionally asking a question, just for clarification's sake. On this day, however, she felt it necessary to contradict Malik's points at every turn.

The professor had been expounding on the events that had recently occurred with the collapse of the Soviet Union, the new independence of the former Soviet satellite states and the reunification of Germany. He asked the students why they thought Soviet empire had collapsed and why the U.S. and its allies had apparently won the Cold War.

Malik raised his hand.

"It seems to me that the Soviet Union was bankrupted by the arms race between itself and us," Malik began.

Ayesha, without raising her hand, interrupted him. "Who is 'us'?" Her voice was sardonic and knowing.

Malik glanced at her. "The United States, of course," he answered mildly.

"I'm not a part of that!" Ayesha shot back. "I didn't try to bankrupt the Soviet Union. The United States government purposely set out to destroy another country. They never asked for my vote when they did this!"

Great...a live one, Malik thought. "My parents are tax-payers and voters. They paid for the arms race with their sweat. They and I are a part of this country. However, if you don't want to be a part of this country, that's up to you. From now on, when I use the first person plural pronouns 'we' and 'us,' I'll make sure that I add except for Miss

Watson. By the way, Miss Watson, do your parents pay taxes?" Malik couldn't help taking a shot at her. He had heard that Ayesha's mother was a single welfare recipient.

"You Uncle Toms are all..."

"Miss Watson, that's enough. You're out of line with the name calling. Mr. Hayes has the floor."

Well, it took you long enough to step in. Malik knew that this professor had the same political leanings that Ayesha did. He was just more polite about it.

"Thank you, sir." Malik continued on his subject, seeming not to be perturbed, but inside, he was boiling. If anyone, *anyone,* threw down the intellectual gauntlet in front of him, he never hesitated to pick it up. But why did it have to be somebody black this time? He especially hated having to put a black person in his/her place, but he would stand up to any challenge set before him.

That it had been a black *woman,* especially set Malik's teeth on edge. When Malik was on the attack, he was ruthless. On the football field, he could deliver a surprisingly vicious block, belying his relatively slim build. On the intellectual field, he was equally as vicious, but unlike when on the football field, he would feel guilty when he made a particularly malevolent stab at another. Having made that crack about Ayesha's mother filled him with remorse and put him in an even worse mood. But, she was asking for it.

Since he had come to NMU, three years ago, most of his dates had been white. Initially, he was fascinated by white girls, the straight blond hair, the different smell, the free and easy manner. But that euphoria had faded. Now he knew that most of them were fascinated by him for a similar reason. They didn't care that he was a three-year senior, didn't care that he loved math. They didn't care that he was funny, or liked old jazz, or about anything like that. They cared about finding out one thing: whether it was true what they said about black men. Malik was a young man and wasn't above getting a little bit if the bait was appealing enough, but for the most part, he was disgusted by the ones who wanted a sample of the dark meat. And many were so obvious about it, that it caused his fertile imagination to take over: he was up on an auction block, being inspected for purchase as a stud.

He knew that a lot of black guys at NMU wouldn't be caught dead with a black girl (not that there were that many to chose from). They were entranced by white girls for the same reasons he had been. Like him, they'd come from all-black environments and had never been near the types of girls that were at NMU. Now, such girls were throwing themselves at them.

Malik also knew that most of these black guys also enjoyed the murderous looks they got from white guys when they sported the blondest and the prettiest of white girls on their arms.

Malik found this incredibly stupid. Why hang out with someone just to annoy somebody else? Is that going to make you some money? Probably lose you some money, when you marry that girl, find out that she's just trying to get back at white people too, doesn't really care about you, divorces you and take half your shit.

Besides, that initial white girl craze had had an unintended side effect on his life: most black girls on the campus hated him. They hated the other black athletes, too, but unlike them, Malik actually cared. He was his usual self with black girls, a friendly extrovert and the comedian. But most gave him a wide berth, lumping him in with the rest of the arrogant athletes. He wasn't surprised at Ayesha's summary judgment of him, but it had hurt him. He had liked her in the beginning and had hoped she'd give him a chance. *No such luck*, he sighed as he walked into the Quad.

And via the classroom incident, he had put a nail in that coffin.

As he walked in, he eyed the lounge chairs. Their high backs prevented a passer-by from seeing who was sitting in them and they appeared to be empty, so Malik decided he would sit down for a couple of minutes and attempt to cool off. As he rounded the corner of one of the seats, he saw that it wasn't empty. Amanda Bain sat there in tears.

Malik fought his first instinct to get back around the chair and be on his way before she saw him. But his better nature won out. *Shoot, the girl was crying. Maybe her mother died or something.*

"Mandy?"

Mandy looked up at him and began to quickly compose herself. "Oh, hi, Malik." The two were silent for a few seconds.

"Um, is there something wrong? Do you...is there something I can help you with?"

"It's not a big deal."

"Well, if you're crying about it, it must be a big deal, at least to you."

Mandy looked at him. She had disliked Malik on sight, having met him through Kevin the year before. And the feeling had seemed to be mutual. Oh, he was always polite and always spoke. He had never treated her the way many of Kevin's black teammates did: eyeing her as a potential bedmate. But whenever she walked up to Kevin, he would beat a hasty retreat and when he did choose to stay around, he would look at her with something she was unaccustomed to seeing in men's eyes: scorn. He treated her as if she were beneath him. *What an asshole,* she remembered thinking.

So, in return, she disliked him right back. Now, here he was. No condescension this time. He seemed to be genuinely concerned. Should she tell him about her and Kevin and that girl? What would Kevin think about her confiding in his best friend? To hell with it.

"Well, Malik, if you must know, I got my heart broke."

Broken, said the English stickler inside Malik's head. He shushed it.

"Well, that always sucks. Anybody I know?"

Mandy made a face at him. "Yes, you know him. Kevin, of course. He found somebody else-that tall, black girl. Pretty, I guess if you like that kind of thing."

Malik's eyes widened in recognition.

"Oh." He paused for a second. "I'm sorry."

"Sorry? Why would you be sorry about me getting hurt?" Her voice was sardonic.

Malik sat down next to her. "Hey, Mandy, I know you and I have never gotten along, but you're hurt. I've never wished anything like that on you."

Mandy sniffed and pushed her hair out of her face. "Malik, *I'm* sorry. I don't have any right to take my bad mood out on you. And, to be honest, I don't have a right to be heart-broken about this Kevin thing. We were just friends."

"But you were hoping it would be something more."

"You got it. That's how I thought it was supposed to happen. You become friends with a guy and then you get together."

"'The best laid plans of mice and men...'"

"'...sometimes go astray.' You read Hemingway?"

"Him and Steinbeck-that's where the quote originally came from," said Malik as his voice trailed off bashfully.

Mandy laughed. "No wonder you're so arrogant and obnoxious-star athlete and a scholar to boot."

"Is that why you act so funny around me? You think I'm obnoxious? I thought it was because you thought you were too high and mighty to associate with us lowly black boys."

She looked him in the eyes. "Malik, give me a break. Sometimes people will dislike you just because you're *you*."

"Oh, so you mean that you were judging me by the content of my character. Thank you!"

They both laughed.

"I always thought you were kind of loud and obnoxious yourself," Malik teased.

"I am. That's why disliked you so much. We're too much alike. I think that's also why Kevin picked that girl over me. I have a tendency to speak my mind a little too much."

"There's nothing wrong with speaking your mind. Personally, I like girls who say what's on their mind. But, everyone might not have that preference," said Malik gently.

Mandy shrugged. "Obviously not." She looked at him. "When you came over here, you didn't look like you were in the best of moods either."

"Definitely not." He told her an abridged version of what had happened in class.

"Sound like this girl is intimidated by you. You are a little intimidating."

"You're intimidated by me?"

"Yes, I guess I was. I guess you're not so bad after all. You did make me laugh on one of the crappiest days of my life." She smiled at him.

"Happy to be of service," he said, reddening slightly.

"You know what? Suddenly, I'm starving."

"Are you asking me to have lunch with you?" he grinned.

"Well, if you're not ashamed to be seen with someone as loud and obnoxious as me."

"Lead on. If you get too loud, I've got a gag in my pocket."

"You can try using it, but you'll have a hard time catching a ball with your arm broke...broken."

Malik laughed delightedly. The two got up and headed for the Quad's cafeteria.

Chapter Eight

In three months, Felice's world had been changed and herself along with it. A new feeling, a sense of *something,* was a part of that world. She hadn't had much experience with the feeling, but she recognized it immediately: happiness. The recognition of happiness underscored its previous absence in her life.

Surely, her new-found happiness had a great deal to do with Kevin, but there was more to it than just his presence in her life. She finally *liked* who she was, not just because Kevin loved her, but because she loved herself and was proud of herself. Her grades were bound to be high.

Why? Because she had put in the time and effort to make them that way. Her relationship with her parents was good. Why? Because she obeyed them and had stopped lying to them. She and her parents actually talked to each other instead of them talking and her listening, or not listening in sullen silence.

Then, on the other hand, Kevin *had* played a major role in her life. The feminists had been wrong about the value of a man in the quality of a woman's life. Evil men, like the Taus, could ruin a woman's life. But only if woman allowed it, as she had. Conversely, good men, like her father and Kevin, could up the quality of life to very high levels.

She started thinking about the girls she knew who didn't have any men in their lives and Adrienne immediately popped up in her mind. Adrienne was tough, powerful, head-strong, and opinionated, but Felice wondered how much of that part of her was just *her* and how much of it was from necessity. Felice had always had her father, her uncles, her male cousins--and now Kevin--around to protect her. And though she had chaffed under her father's occasional over-protectiveness, she was secretly pleased by it, and knew that it was a demonstration of his love for her.

On top of that, she had only to recall her involvement with the Taus to understand why her father was the man he was.

Who did Adrienne have to do that, Felice asked herself. No one. So, she and Laura had to protect themselves. And they did an admirable job of it too, and being six-footers hadn't hurt, either. She herself had been the beneficiary of Adrienne's tough, powerful persona.

But it seemed to Felice, that women without men in their lives, had to often take on the duties that a man would usually have, were he present, able, and willing. Felice recalled a conversation she had with Adrienne about Laura and how tough she was.

Laura, after having caught one of her perspective suitors about to rape her daughter, had subsequently refused to date at all until her daughter left home. (Felice had privately wondered where Laura had buried the body.) But since Adrienne had grown tall and strong enough to take care of most attackers, her mother would occasionally go out to dinner with a guy. Laura had never brought any of them home, however.

"Mom says that none of them had yet earned the honor of crossing her threshold. She means that in a variety of ways, knowing her," Adrienne had explained.

"Adrienne, are you gay?"

The question had just popped out of her mouth, unpremeditated. Now, as she remembered the conversation in relationship to her present train of thought, she knew why.

Adrienne had looked at her best friend with years of pain on her face. "No, I'm not, and thanks for asking."

"I'm sorry, I didn't mean anything..."

"Felice, I've had many people think this about me. What six-foot, basketball-playing woman wouldn't have that thought about her? Heck, a good portion of my teammates are."

Felice had raised her hand in protest. "I don't want to know who."

"Nor, would I tell you. Whether they want their preferences known or not is their business, not mine. Felice, before you beat yourself up too much about this, I'm glad to know that you would still hang out with me, while suspecting that I might be a lesbian. That say's a lot about you."

Felice had looked at her. "The stereotype strikes again."

"Yes, it does." Adrienne had sighed. "Back when I started playing ball, my mother told me that this would be so. Her ability to tell the future is so annoying ...." Felice laughed.

"But that didn't make it hurt any less when the subject first started coming up. After I had been playing ball a while though, I saw why it was a stereotype. Stereotypes become stereotypes because they are, mostly, based in fact. A big, tough woman, who plays sports, often wants to sleep with other women."

"But not in your case."

"No, I'm an exception to that rule; not that it gets me any dates. But, girl, I'll be straight with you. (Hey, that's a joke.) Several of my teammates are quite envious of my relationship with you."

The look of disgust on Felice's face was strong. Adrienne laughed. "Don't worry. I am here to assure you that I like my humans on three legs." Both women broke up with laughter.

"That boyfriend of my mother's wasn't the first one to try something with me. When I started playing ball, my mother told me to tell her when the first coach hit on me. It didn't take long. I was ten and five-seven. As it happens, that coach was a woman. I told my mom right away, told her what the woman's name was and guess what Laura did? She found out where the woman lived, went to her house, and threatened to cut every appendage of hers off and stuff 'em down her throat if she so much as looked at me cross-eyed."

"As different-thinking as you mother is, I would have thought that she wouldn't have problems with lesbians, or specifically, with you being one."

"Actually, she said that she wouldn't have a problem with it, if it were *my* choice. She just didn't want me to be coerced into it as a child.

"Mom actually has quite a few homosexual friends. Heck, she's an artist living in Santa Fe; she couldn't avoid that. She says she even considered becoming a lesbian when I was small. I recall seeing a few rather mannish looking women over the house when I was a kid, but none of them have been over in years."

"She considered *becoming* one? I'm not an expert but I don't think it works that way. Did you ask her why she wanted to do that? Be a lesbian I mean."

"Didn't have to. You met my mom. She'll tell you the truth in a split second. She said that nearly all of them had been molested by either men or women when they were kids. She thought that it was their psychological reaction to child-abuse.

"She stopped having them over to the house, because she found that she didn't want to 'become' a lesbian, and she also discovered that being around them wasn't good for her. She said that they were some of the most self-absorbed people that she'd ever been around, either because they hated themselves for what they did, or because all they cared about was the next time they were going to get laid."

"Sound like your mom ought to be teaching a psych course at NMU or somewhere."

"Are you nuts? She'd be booted out in the first semester, if not before. And not just for telling truths that nobody wants to hear. Mom's not exactly a team-player."

"Guess that's why she's an artist."

"Exactly. There was another reason, the main reason, that Mom stopped the funny girls from coming over to the house. She would watch how they would look at me. She said they would have a predator's gleam in their eyes. She then knew it was time to make some changes."

"Wow! Laura is pretty radical."

"Yep. And she's a mother hen to the max. It gets on my nerves a lot of times, but I know it's because she loves me."

"You're all she has."

Adrienne stopped and looked at Felice. Then she sighed. "Yeah, I guess you're right."

"You know what my mom told me about having children? She said that the choice of having a child is a debt that you owe the child, and that when you have a baby, you're responsible for everything that person becomes; not just for eighteen years but for the rest of the person's life. Maybe that's why Laura is so protective of you. She knows what her job is."

"Whew, it's getting too deep around here! Hey, girl, you and me are teenagers. Aren't we supposed to be talking about boys or make-up or clothes or some other stupid shit like that?"

"Only, if we were the boring airheads that we both dog out all the time."

"Guess that's why neither of us can get a real date. Oops, I forgot about you and Kevin."

"Do you ever hear from your father?"

The smile had dropped from Adrienne's face and she pressed her lips together tightly, thinning them to near invisibility. "Nope and don't want to. He's had almost twenty years to at least attempt to be a real father. His time has run out."

The feminist were wrong, Felice decided. Roles weren't interchangeable. People made adjustments and adaptations to the life that circumstances hand them, but gender roles weren't interchangeable. Women, and sometimes men (like Kevin's father), had to deal with losses and abandonment, and dealt with them well, but there would still be consequences, good or bad.

Felice stopped in mid-thought. She wondered whether Laura Anderson and Herbert Hart would like each other.

* * *

The party was a success. With the serendipity of March first being the birthday of both Herbert Hart and Joseph LeCroix, both of their children were able to maneuver the two into a party at the LeCroix household. Herbert had met Felice before and was enchanted with her—or so it seemed to Kevin. Since father and son had spent so many years living in a totally masculine environment, it was difficult for Kevin to be sure.

When Felice and Kevin hatched the birthday party plan, she had made sure to invite the Andersons. It was a first time meeting for all of the adults and Herbert Hart and Laura Anderson did indeed like each other. The two spent two hours on the LeCroix patio laughing at each others jokes.

All clean up was done by Felice, Kevin, Joey, and Adrienne and afterward, the older offspring went to take in a movie while Joey went down the street to the home of one of his little league teammates. With all company having departed and no work to be done, Joseph and Vetra had taken the place of Herbert and Laura on the patio.

"Not too bad, eh? This birthday, I mean," said Vetra.

"Yes, my love, this was one of my better birthdays," he pecked her on the cheek. "Especially so, considering I didn't have to cook and the food was not Creole."

"But the cake was baked by one," said Vetra. "That was Richard's birthday present—that, and holding down the fort at the Experience."

"That's my brother. He's always been a better baker than me." The two sat silently for a bit.

"I love you, Joe."

"I love you too, Mrs. LeCroix—especially for not saying some form of 'I told you so.'"

"About what?" she asked.

"About giving that kid—Kevin-a chance. He and his father are good people."

"There was no reason for me to say 'I told you so' about that. You should be saying that to me. You're a lot less stubborn than I had thought you were all these years." Joseph gave his wife a look.

"I'm not sure whether that's a compliment or not."

"It's a slam against me for not seeing it."

Joseph shook his head laughing. "Excellent recovery. But, I was wrong about them—wrong to see them as part of a group rather than as individuals."

"Well, honey, I won't say 'I told you so.' I'll say that you are the good man that I married, and you're just demonstrating it right now."

"So, what's my reward?"

She grinned. "You'll see this Friday."

* * *

"What about the *Prince of Tides*?"

"Already seen it."

"*Fried Green Tomatoes*?"

"What? Do you have some perverse love of chick-flicks?

"Not in the least. But I thought you might, being a chick and all."

Mandy grinned at Malik—or rather she grinned at the receiver as she sat on her bed talking to him on the telephone. "Aren't you the one who dislikes stereotypes?"

"Yes, but in the case of women, all of them are true."

"Well, Mr. Double-Standard, it just so happens that you're wrong this time. I will sometimes check out the occasional chick-flick—if it has good reviews—but I like fun movies better. Action, blood, and guts, sci-fi--"

"You like sci-fi?" Malik was excited. "Have you seen *Star Trek VI* yet? Please tell me you haven't."

"I haven't. I don't know of anyone who is enough of a dork to go with me."

"Well you do now, Chica! I've been meaning to see it since it came out in December, but I had the same problem... nobody to go with."

"I heard that it's a Cold War allegory," said Mandy.

"How so?"

"It's a rapprochement between the Klingons and the Federation is all I know. It explains how Worf got on the

Enterprise D in Next Generation. I even know that the guy who plays Worf is in the movie."

Malik was grinning. "So," he began playfully. "How many conventions have you been to?"

"I'm not answering."

"What did you go as? Yeoman Rand? A green belly dancer?"

"An Andorian."

Malik burst out laughing. "Now that's a picture I'd pay money to own."

"I was allergic to the blue make-up so I didn't show my face for a week afterward."

"Mandy, I have to say that I'm impressed by this side of you."

"What, I'm not as boring as you thought I was?"

"To be honest, that's it exactly."

"Well, hon, you *are* as arrogant as I thought you were but I like it."

"Damn, you sure know how to sweet talk a brother. So, what about the late afternoon showing on Friday and then maybe we can get something to eat afterward?"

"That sounds great." *Quickly*, she said to herself in a split second, *before he asks*. "Let's meet at the theater."

"Okay. I'll look at the paper, figure out what time and tell you tomorrow at lunch."

"Okay, bud." She didn't want to hang up but she had some studying to accomplish. "I'll see you tomorrow. Good night."

"Good night, Amanda."

She hung up and sat there for a few seconds as Malik's last word echoed in her mind. There was something about the way Malik had said her name. Not 'Mandy,' but *Amanda*. Whatever that something was, hours later, it caused her to fall asleep easily, while for the first time in months, giving no thought whatsoever to Kevin Hart.

Chapter Nine

"Are you going to the A.S.U. dinner next Saturday?" asked Adrienne. She and Felice were sitting in an almost empty Quad. Being mid-afternoon, most students were studying, working.

"No!"

"And, why not?" Adrienne asked knowingly.

"Hello? You know why not. My reputation, of course."

"Yeah, right. You know it's not because of that. It's because of Kevin."

Felice sighed. "Well, that's the main reason. I wouldn't go there without Kevin and I know they would probably give him hell.

"Kevin's a big boy. You ought to let him decide if he wants to catch a little hell or not."

Adrienne paused for a beat, and then continued. "Stop being so fearful and live your life for yourself and to hell with everybody else. Remember what Laura said? Fear is the opposite of love."

"You and Laura have been watching too many *Kung Fu* reruns," Felice snorted.

"Are you ashamed of Kevin?"

"Are you kidding? Of course not. I am just not sure if *I'm* up for the challenge of what we'll have to deal with if we go to that dinner. Sure, we get looks on campus and around town. Heck, if you remember, on our first date, some stupid white people tried to loud-talk us."

"But you're just not sure if you want to walk in the lion's den on purpose."

"That's it exactly. You know how *we* are, Adrienne. Oh, sure an occasional white person, like that couple might be brave enough to say something, but usually, they'll keep their mouths shut."

"That's not what my mother says she went through."

"But it's not 1965 or even 1975 anymore. The tables have turned."

"True. I remember, when I was a little kid, we got more negative comments from black people than whites. Actually, most white people would tell my mother what a beautiful child I was." Adrienne tossed her head in mock vanity.

"And you were all too ready to agree," Felice grinned.

"But you know and I know that some of the people there--black people--won't be so hesitant to say what's on what passes for their minds."

"Right."

"So, you'll let them keep you from going."

Felice said nothing.

"You let them say stuff behind your back like, 'guess that hoochie Felice was too chicken to bring that white boy in here.'"

"Adrienne..."

"'Guess she knew how far to go than to bring that peckerwood around here. I wish she *woulda* brought that fool up in here. I'da showed her how white boys and race-traitors are *supposed* to be treated.'"

Felice looked at her with some exasperation. "Boy, you've sure changed your tune about Kevin. Seems to me that you were nearly singing the race-traitor song not too long ago, when I was thinking of going out with him."

"Yeah, well I was wrong."

"Oh my God! Call the newspapers!" Felice said, enjoying the moment.

Adrienne sucked her teeth. "You'd better call 'em, 'cause it doesn't happen too much.

"I was wrong about Kevin and white guys in general. My mom does give good advice, but occasionally, she let's her own problems with people cloud her thinking. Not usually, but when she does, it's usually pretty bad."

"It seems like the fruit doesn't fall too far from the tree."

"Okay! Stop rubbing it in my face. Anyway, just like it's wrong for other people to judge a black person by the actions of another black person, it's wrong for black people to do the same to somebody else. That includes white men."

"What changed your mind?"

"You and Kevin, to be honest. He's a good guy."

Felice smiled. "Yes."

"And one other person—Kevin's dad."

"His dad? What does Mr. Hart have to do with this?"

"Let's just say that Laura has been cutting more than one white guy a break."

"Really?" Felice was happy. "That must have got started at my house. That's so cool. Your mom and Kevin's dad are both the best."

"Yep, two guys in one family treating women with respect and love.

"And on the opposite side, there are the Taus, our 'brothers,' treating us--both you and I--like the slaves our ancestors were.   Yep, the tables have turned for sure."

"So true."

"So, back to the subject: what are you going to do about the dinner?"

"You *know* that I don't want to go"

"Neither do I." said Felice.

"Yes, you do." Felice looked at Kevin then sighed.

"Yes, I do, because…"

"Because you aren't going to let anyone keep you out of any place that you have a right to be; because you don't believe in fear."

"Yes, I do," she grinned.

"Well, okay," Kevin grinned back, "but my dad says this about fear: 'feel it, but do what needs to be done anyway. Don't let fear rule you. And besides," he began with a slanted grin. "You want to get revenge on the Taus. I do too. Not because of anything they've done to me, obviously, but because of you."

"I don't deserve any revenge. I just want to be happy and I'm happy with you." Kevin put his arm around her and put his cheek against her forehead.

"That's the exact revenge I had in mind, darlin'. They tried to hurt you and you didn't stay hurt...too bad and so sad for them."

"So, what about you big guy? You afraid to go in there?" It was Kevin's turn to give Felice a straight glance.

"Don't ever ask me if I'm afraid to do something, Felice. Because even if I am, I'm not going to tell you or anyone else."

"Understood."

Felice got the sense that she was hearing something of great import come out of Kevin's mouth, something more than a self-description. It was a portend of—something, but of what?

It wouldn't be long before she found out.

They arrived at the A.C.C. at six-thirty p.m. sharp. Dinner was at seven and the ceremonies began at eight-fifteen. Felice had described the gathering as a "we love us because we're doing such a good job" party. What that job—that objective—was, Felice still wasn't sure. She knew no more about African heritage than when she first became aware of the A.C.C. But since she had been a part of its functioning in that oh-so-innocent first year, she would take her bow.

Stepping over the threshold of the dining room, Felice drew what she thought was a near-silent intake of breath. But as she did so, Kevin briefly smiled down at her and ran his hand over hers—which was tucked under his left arm. As they entered the almost-full room all, eyes turned to look at them.

"I didn't think she would do it. I didn't think that stupid broad had the nerve to bring *him* in here," said Kim Adams scornfully. Vonetta glared at her.

"Why shouldn't she? He's her man."

"Why don't you hate..." Kim trailed off as she watched Vonetta's back recede, then her eyes began to widen as it became obvious where Vonetta was heading.

Felice and Kevin had begun to make their way toward an open table when Vonetta rounded another table and stopped in front of her, which, in turn, stopped Felice immediately in her tracks. The two young women seemed to be transfixed by each other until Felice broke the spell.

"How have you been, Vonetta?"

"I've been great. What about you?"

"Great also." They paused. Kevin, who didn't know of the enmity between the two, sensed something important about to happen, nevertheless, and watched in silence.

Vonetta seemed to be propelled by an unseen force, a force that she wanted to resist, but couldn't.

"Why don't you and Kevin come and sit with us? Calvin and I, and two other couples are there, and we have

great seats-right in the middle so we can see if someone
starts acting crazy."

Felice looked at Vonetta with a relieved and grateful
smile. "Okay?" she checked with Kevin.

"Okay," he agreed.

As they followed where Vonetta lead, a particular set of
eyes would have burned holes in Kevin's back if they could
have. Instead, the mind behind those eyes had to be content
with watching and waiting.

At the table, those who didn't know each other
introduced themselves. Calvin and Kevin gave each other
the man handshake and Kim, who had been cutting Felice
down before, was all smiles and graciousness--something
about which Vonetta made a mental note.

Felice didn't even feel uncomfortable at greeting
Calvin. It was obvious that he and Vonetta had eyes only for
each other. Reflecting on that, Felice felt the tiniest twinge of
regret about her behavior, but it dissipated. All had turned
out well for all concerned.

What none of them seem to be cognizant of was that
all the other dinner guests in the room could barely

concentrate on any part of their meals. For good or ill, Kevin and Felice were the stars of the show.

How could they get him outside, mused Trevor as he watched all the ignorant Negroes in the room fawn over that abomination in the middle of it? However, his internal questioning was rhetorical. *Of course it is.* He turned to Andre Carter.

"We'll wait until he goes to drain his lizard, small though it may be. Then we'll give the signal."

"Sounds like a plan."

"What you and I will do is crowd him out the back door. The other brothers will follow our lead."

"Do we want to get him before he goes in to take a piss or afterward."

"Before, of course. I'd like to see the devil piss his pants." They laughed low.

"And when we get him out there?" asked Andre.

"We will discuss things with the man...let him know where his boundaries lie...what he can and cannot do. Oh I'm sure that that devil is used to doing what and who he wants, and Massa can visit the slave quarters all he likes.

But, he cannot flaunt his racism by coming into a gathering like this one."

Yes, thought Andre. *Maybe when we take care of that Cracka I'll have to have a piece of his pie.*

"I can't wait," he said.

"Yes, you can. We all can. Patience is the strength of African peoples. One day we won't have to teach these types of lessons because one of us will be high up enough to ensure that all the enemies of the black African man know their place—maybe that teacher will even be in the White House."

"I can't even imagine that."

"Watch and see. It won't be a very long time from now. But before the general arrives, we have to be the foot soldiers for the cause—for Black Liberation."

The two were so distracted by this conversation that their quarry almost gave them the slip—but not quite. Kevin got into the men's room too fast for them, however, and all dreams of making him urinate on himself were lost. Nonetheless, Trevor gave the appropriate signal and all of the Tau fraternity brothers under his control swiftly made their move to the door. It was a move they had practiced.

Calvin was not among them, being Trevor's "big brother," but he knew a Tau action when he saw one, and for a few minutes--but only a few--wondered against whom the action could be.

"Felice LeCroix." The announcer pronounced Felice's last name correctly--something she was unused to. Kevin was out of his chair before she was in order to pull back her chair. She smiled at him briefly and then walked to the stage to receive her plaque for her volunteer clerical work at the A.C.C.

After the shake-and-take, and as she made her way back to the table, someone began to clap and soon the whole room was clapping. Felice blushed furiously and sat as Kevin pulled out her chair.

It had been Trevor who had started the applause.

"Why in the heck were they applauding me? They didn't do it for anyone else."

"Some smart aleck started it to be funny, I bet," said Vonetta.

"Well, babe," said Kevin, "if it makes you feel any better, that was me whistling."

"You're so sweet. Thank you." Felice gave him a peck on the lips, stirring up a wave of tittering in the vicinity of their side of the table.

"What the..." Kevin began and then cut himself off as he turned to look at the faces which had just observed the kiss. The verdict: a toss-up; one between loathing and longing. That's what Kevin saw in those faces. He looked at Felice.

"Whoa! It's getting weird in here. These folks are freaking out because you kissed me."

"I'm beginning to wonder whether it was such a good idea to come to this dinner," she said.

"Remember this, beautiful: don't ever let anyone keep you out of any place that you want to go."

"You're right. Okay."

"And speaking of going, I'll be right back." Kevin caused another wave of tittering by kissing her this time.

:::::*time to make that move:::* said the signal. And they did.

Kevin stepped out of the men's room into what seem to be an impromptu football game in the back of the A.C.C.

ballroom. Four large men managed to get him out of the back door while holding him up in order to keep him from falling. It was clear that the young men had practiced this move and were used to their prey reacting in a certain manner. But Kevin, being an All-American, a quarterback, and a very large one to boot, managed to whirl out of the enclosure they had been trying to form around him with their bodies. However, he didn't make an attempt to get back in through the doorway—they were blocking it at any rate--or to escape by any other means.

He looked at them. "Um, can I help you...gentlemen?"

One of them stepped forward and looked him in the eye. "Why yes, Kevin Hart, yes you can. My name is Trevor Mason and I just want to tell you that you have no right to be here—especially not with an African woman."

"Kevin's been gone a while," Vonetta noticed.

"That's strange, he has. I wonder if he got to talking to somebody," said Felice.

All of a sudden Calvin stood up, excused himself and ran to the back of the ballroom. Vonetta and Felice looked at each other.

Calvin had disappeared. But minutes later he reappeared and his deep, booming baritone carried throughout the room.

"Everybody that can needs to come out here and see what's going on. Come on!" he gestured. "Come on."

And they did--dozens of them. The ones who were able to get outside through the doorway and who saw and heard the back and forth between Trevor and Kevin, began a chant: NO RACISTS, NO RACISTS, NO RACISTS—and the chant was joined by the rest, even those who could not see what was going on.

It was Calvin who had started the chant, and having accomplished his self-appointed task, he made his way back to his table where Felice and Vonetta still sat, in spite of his exhortation. He bent to whisper something in Vonetta's ear and that got her moving.

"Come on, Felice! It's Kevin and Trevor!"

Before she could react, the three were up and knifing their way through the crowd. Because they were led by Calvin, members of the crowd made way for them until the three got through the doorway and outside the building.

When Felice saw Kevin, she ran to him to hug him. He lifted her easily off the ground and gave her a big kiss, to the cheering delight of the on-lookers. Afterward, they changed their chant to: GO TIGERS, GO TIGERS, GO TIGERS!!

Chapter Ten

"A field trip for the entire weekend? I don't know."

"Come on, Dad. It's for my elective; History of New Mexico. Here's all the paper work. I pay for the trip to and back and I'll drive. The school pays for the hotel. I'd like to see Santa Fe again."

"You mean *I* pay for the trip to and back. And tell me again why I should trust you."

"Because I've been trustworthy, lately. Are you going to make me pay for my past actions forever? Is this like having a felony on your record?"

"You've been hanging out with that Hart kid too much. What a son of a lawyer!"

Felice rolled her eyes. "So, Daddy, is it yes or no?"

"Don't pressure me, girl. I could just say no."

"Okay, Joe. Stop making her twist in the wind." Vetra stepped out from the kitchen, where she had not so secretly been eavesdropping.

"But I was having so much fun." Joseph signed the consent form.

Felice kissed her father on the cheek. "Thanks, Daddy. I won't make you sorry."

"Yeah, yeah, we'll see."

"So, you're going to be gone for two days."

"Yep. Long enough for Mandy to sink those blood-red talons of hers into you."

They sat on a bench near the Quad.

"Be serious. Besides, she'd leave makeup all over my shirt." Felice playfully slapped him on the side of his head.

"Ouch! Could you let me go get my helmet the next time you do that? You've got hands like a boxer," he teased.

"And your head's going to feel like a punching bag if you keep messing with me about Miss Mandy."

"I live in anticipation," he growled as he stole a kiss from her. "Anyway, I think that she and Malik might have something going on."

"You're kidding me! I thought Miss Scarlet, uh, Miss Mandy, didn't consort with us darkies."

"You're being unfair, now. It was never that she didn't like black people. It was just that she didn't like *you.*

"Okay, fine. So Mandy's the second coming of Eleanor Roosevelt."

"I'm not so sure she'd like that comparison," he grinned. "Give the girl a break. There was some competition. You won, she lost. Be generous in your victory."

"Oh, now aren't we the egomaniac, Mr. Prize?

He smiled sweetly at her. "I'm a jock, darlin'. It comes with the territory. Back to Mandy and Malik. I think he's good for her."

"How so?"

"She's softer now; nicer than she used to be. I don't know if it has anything to do with Malik or not, but I think it does. As for him, I have to say this: it's having a good effect on him, too.

"So how come I'm just now finding out about this?"

"I knew you didn't like her and with good reason, though..."

"What?"

"I realize that a lot of the dislike between you is my fault. I did lead her on."

"You made her think you were interested in her."

Kevin grimaced. "Yes." He sighed. "I used her interest in me to help me with my classes."

Felice ran her hand through his hair. "It's good you can admit this. And maybe...just maybe, I can also be big enough to cut her some slack. After all, if Malik likes her, she can't be too bad."

"Back to Malik's interesting effect on her: she seems much more...real."

"I bet her parents aren't too happy about this."

"I don't think her mother knows about it. Malik said that she isn't...not quite as enlightened as the rest of us."

"Well I hope, for both their sakes, that everything goes well. I might even consent to going out one evening with them. How's that for being a generous victor?"

"I'm proud of you, baby."

"So what other trouble are you going to get into while I'm gone?"

"No trouble at all." He looked at her slyly. "Actually I was thinking of taking a drive. Santa Fe's nice this time of year."

Felice was alarmed. "Oh, no you don't! I told my dad that I wasn't up to any monkey business. Please don't make me into a liar. He's just starting to trust me again. Please, Kevin."

"You can't help it if I just happen to show up in Santa Fe on the same weekend you happen to be there."

"What if your dad goes to the restaurant that weekend and happens to let slip that you're up in Santa Fe? What then, huh, genius?"

"Easy. I'll just take my camping gear and tell Dad that me and some of the guys are headed to the mountains to camp out for the weekend. It just so happens that some of them are doing just that."

"You'd lie to your father just like that?"

"Only for an important cause like this-so we can spend some time alone together, without one or more of our parents watching us like hawks, especially *your* father."

"You have a point." She cocked her head at him. "So, genius, what are we going to do together up there in Santa Fe all alone?"

"Thank you for acknowledging my tremendous mental abilities, darlin'. We'll lose your teacher and your classmates. Then we'll...see the sights."

"You make sure you bring all your...gear...with you. The camping gear, I mean."

He stood up and gave her a snappy salute.

"Yes, Ma'am!"

* * *

After visiting Laura Anderson and having dinner with her classmates, Felice headed back to her room. Some of her classmates were headed out to sample Santa Fe's rather considerable night life, which including, Felice knew all too well, drinking and smoking--cigarettes and otherwise. With her promise to Joseph in mind, she bade them goodnight, pleading that she had a test to study for.

But there was a thought knawing at her mind: *Kevin could be here tonight.* She thought of how it might be making love to him. Would it be any different from making love to a black man? Kissing was definitely different, with Kevin's lips being thinner than she was used to. His smell was also different. Not better or worse--just different.

Come on, LeCroix, stop avoiding it. Racial differences in love-making weren't important and they weren't what she should be thinking about. What she should be thinking about was her promise to her father. How could she make love with Kevin with that in mind? And what about Kevin? If she declined making love to him, how would he react? Would he feel as though she lead him on? Would he throw her past in her face?

She remembered her flings. They weren't all that they had been cracked up to be. According to all the latest literature, sex was supposed to be this phenomenal thing to be indulged in at whim, by consenting adults, "safely," of course. But only with Calvin and Daniel had things been moderately pleasurable though with both, she had on some level, felt as though she were second choice.

She supposed that what little pleasure she felt when having sex with either of them was tied to the fact that she had cared about them. What had her mother said? *Be careful about who you let into your heart.* That was the real meaning of safe sex: be in love and be sure that the other person loves you.

She remembered watching a TV preacher expound on this subject. Felice would never watch the local Christian station with her parents around for fear that they would begin pressuring her to resume attending Mass with them. She still wasn't sure how she felt about God, but watching some of the preachers on TV and thinking about what they said, had given her a sense of peace. Sure, some of them seemed to be hungry only for money, but others seemed intent on preaching the word of God and getting that message to the greatest amount of people possible. And what was money anyway, but a tool? They used their "tools" to get their message out to people like her.

"When a man and woman are joined together in matrimony," the preacher had paraphrased from the Bible, "the two become one flesh. So, when you give yourself physically to another, you become one with that person, physically and spiritually. That's why there's so much pain and anguish concerning so-called love relationships these days. People are becoming 'one flesh' with dozens of others. And when the person they've given a part of themselves to leaves, and the next leaves, and the next, that person's spirit is being chipped away just a little bit at a time. After years of this, that person is a spiritual and emotional cripple."

Well ain't that the truth, she remembered thinking. How empty and stupid she had felt after her fiasco with the

Taus! And after Daniel's betrayal, she had felt as though someone had tried to rip her intestines out. She knew for certain that she didn't want that to happen with her and Kevin. He was more than just a boyfriend, he was her *friend.* He knew nearly everything about her and he still liked her. *No, LeCroix, he* loves *you. And you love him.*

She didn't just want to have sex with him, she wanted to make love to him; she wanted to be a part of him and she wanted him to be a part of her. That's what was missing with the others, even with Daniel and Calvin. They were using her, of course, but the fact was this: she was using them, as well. She had been using them all, not only physically, but emotionally--to make herself feel more beautiful; desirable. They desired, all right, but it wasn't *her* they desired, not the real her. Did any of them ask about her hobbies or her plans for the future like Kevin did the first time they met? Did she ask those things of them? Did they tease her or tell her jokes? Did she do that with them? Had she talked with any of them about God? Did she even know whether they believed in God or not?

She was just as guilty as they were of treating them like mere bodies. That's what the phrase "getting a piece" really meant. However, it was really a piece of one's self, one's soul, which one gives away when one has sex with another; when it's cheapened or dismissed as a biological function, like going to the bathroom, and both parties suffer. She knew that only too well.

Her thoughts turned back to Kevin. If he brought up the Taus, then that would tell her what she needed to know about him.

She decided she would tell him what she had just been thinking about, in an honest and straight-forward way. That was all there was to it.

She was awakened by a knock on the door. Still fully clothed, she jumped off of the bed, took a glance at her face and hair, and then went to look through the peep-hole on the door. There he was with flowers in hand. For a brief second, she toyed with the idea of pretending not to be there, but the impulse passed. She took a deep breath then opened the door.

"Hi, darlin'." Kevin stepped through the doorway.

"Hi," Felice answered. Kevin looked at her, sensing that something was amiss. He handed her the flowers and kissed her lightly on the lips.

"Red roses," she observed, smiling briefly and taking a whiff. "I know I saw a vase in here. There it is." She picked the vase up from the dresser and went into the bathroom to fill it with water. "I wonder if there's anything in here that I can use to cut the stems off. That with make them last longer."

"That's right. Here, I have a pocket knife. I'll do it." He took the roses from her, cut the stems expertly and set the roses inside the vase. "Where do you want them?"

"On the dresser to one side, so I can look at them and smell them in the morning when I'm getting ready." Felice watched, amused, as he set the vase down and made a joking show of getting them at just the correct spot. He then turned to face her.

"Aren't you happy to see me?"

"Kevin...I'm always happy to see you."

"But not here and not right now."

"Let's sit down." There was a small love seat in the room. They sat and he put his arm around her and pulled her to him. She responded in kind and then both of them relaxed and just sat still, her head on his shoulder and his chin resting lightly on her head. They were quiet for a few minutes.

He broke the silence. "You're not ready for this, are you?"

"No. Please don't be angry with me. Please."

He sat her up to look into her face. "Felice, tell me. Why do you think that I would be angry at you about not being ready to make love?"

"Because of my past. You know that I'm not exactly a dewy-fresh, blushing virgin. In case you don't know the whole story, I have an ugly reputation."

"Well, if you do, the news is not spreading like wildfire around campus. I do know something about it. Those creeps at the dinner tried to tell me some things after they gang-blocked me out the back door."

Felice's eyes got wide.

"Calm down, baby. I told them I already knew about it because you had told me, which you had, even though you didn't give me any details. And I told them to get the hell out of my face. I don't want to know the details. It has nothing to do with you and me, nothing to do with our relationship."

"But, I....I wouldn't blame you if you felt as though....felt as if I were....slighting you in some way..."

"Okay, let's be straight about this, like we are about everything else. You thought that I would get mad if you didn't make love with me, because you had made love with whomever else. You thought that I would think that you felt that I wasn't good enough for you or whatever.

"Felice. Whatever else you and I are to each other, we're friends. If we're going to be lovers too, it has to be the right time and the right place for *both* of us. And I honestly do not care what went on between you and some jackass who was too stupid to hold onto you."

"There was more than one."

"So what. I ain't no blushin' virgin either. Do you want to hear about my adventures?"

"No, because I couldn't care less."

"And that's exactly the way I feel about your situation."

She looked at him warmly. "You're so wonderful," she said after she kissed him gently.

"Now, don't try to start anything now," he grinned. "I'm not that kinda guy."

"I want to tell you about what I was thinking before you got here, not about the guys, but about...love making and....how it should be."

He was still grinning. "Now don't get too graphic or you're going to start put ideas in my head again."

"No, silly, I mean I was thinking about what should be going on between two people before they make love, how they should feel about each other and themselves."

"Okay."

"Well, it seems to me that if the two people don't love each other when they make love, it becomes just like eating when you're hungry. It has no more meaning than that.

"But when you do love the person you're making love with, it seems like both might get more out of it than just the physical pleasure."

"Their spirits join together along with their bodies."

She looked at him. "That's exactly what I was thinking. I don't really know from personal experience, though."

"Neither do I. But I think I've seen two people like that before. I've seen it in my grandparents-my mom's parents. They still kiss and hold hands and pat each other on the butt."

She laughed. "That's so cool. I see that in my parents, too. Your grandparents must really, really love each other." She paused and then spoke gently. "I can't imagine what it must have been like for them after losing your mom."

"They...were...torn up. My dad told me once that he thought they were going to get a divorce. This was after almost forty years of marriage."

"I read somewhere that most couples do divorce after they lose a child, no matter how old that child is."

"Yep. But they kept it together. It's fun now to watch two old farts act like teenagers.

"Kevin."

He nuzzled his face into her hair. "Yes, darlin'."

"What was your mother like?"

Kevin lifted his head up, looked at her then looked up into the ceiling. He began slowly.

"She was real tall, around six feet with dark brown hair and hazel eyes. Sigourney Weaver reminds me a lot of her. Both Dad and I have a lot of trouble watching her movies." He took his arm from around Felice and clasped his hands between his knees. Felice watched his face as its youth was subsumed by memory and sadness.

"She and Dad and I used to do all sorts of things together. She couldn't sit still. We'd camp and hunt. She and Dad were serious activists, too. Oh she didn't care about saving whales or deer or birds. She cared about humans, cared about things like apartheid and gang violence and abortion and drugs and alcohol abuse. It's a joke that she was killed by a drunk driver...a sick one." He paused, seeming to collect himself.

Felice reached up to caress him on the shoulder. "If it's too hard for you, honey, we can talk about something else."

"No. I need to talk about her," he said as he turned to look at her. "There's been so much silence about Mom between me and my dad. It's almost like she was never here and I just popped up out of the blue. I've tried to talk with him about it. I *need* to talk about her, and I know that he does, too. But I think that he's afraid that he'll lose control if he does. I think that he thinks that he needs to be strong for me."

"You two need to lean on each other."

"And we do in a lot of ways, but that one subject is nearly never talked about. I was totally shocked when he mentioned about my grandparents almost getting divorced after it happened, but when I tried to draw him out about it, he changed the subject."

"How old were you then?"

"Sixteen."

"Maybe now that you're grown and now that a little more time has passed, he's ready. Tell me more about her. What was her name?"

"Carla. Carla Josephine Walker Hart. That was my mother's name."

"It feels good for you to say her name. I can tell."

"Yes, it does." He turned to look at her again. "It feels good to remember that she was here. And it feels good to talk about her with you."

The two sat talking about Carla Hart and lots of other things until two-thirty in the morning. When they both finally wore out, they stretched out on the bed, fully-clothed, and fell asleep in each others' arms.

They were awakened four hours later by the alarm that Felice had set before Kevin had arrived. Felice had coffee sent to the room, and they drank and laughed and joked easily while getting ready to go. Felice showered while Kevin, who had rented a room on his own, went to take his shower.

Felice walked Kevin to his car and kissed him good-bye. Her trip mates eyed the two curiously and ribbed each other lewdly, speculating on what must have went on in her room the previous night.

Chapter Eleven

After her last class the following Monday, Felice headed home with the events of the weekend swirling in her head. What had she done to deserve a guy like Kevin? Conversely, she felt a sense of guilt, as well. What would her father say if he found out about the visit, regardless of the outcome? He'd flip out, of course. He'd never believe that she and Kevin spent a chaste evening talking about his deceased mother or that they had slept together, barely touching each other and fully clothed.

She suddenly realized that she had turned left instead of the usual right toward Interstate 40, which would take her home. This right turn would take her toward...the restaurant. That was it. Her only course of action was to tell her father the whole story and take the consequences. He might be angry enough to forbid her from seeing Kevin, but he couldn't say that she had lied to him or tried to hide the truth from him. She at least owed him that.

She pulled her car up a block down from the restaurant. She figured that, since it was about one-thirty, the lunch crowd should be thinning out. Ever since "LeCroix's" had received a glowing review in the *Albuquerque Mirror* two years prior, the restaurant had a steady following. Additionally, since her father and her uncle Richard had moved from it's southeast location to be closer to NMU hospital and many other businesses, LeCroix's had gotten the benefit of that clientele. If there were still too many customers inside, she might have to wait until her father wasn't too busy to talk to her. Perhaps, she could get Uncle Richard to take care of things while they sat in the office and talked. Hopefully there were enough customers in the restaurant to keep Joseph from making too much noise when she broke the news to him.

The block stroll was like a death march to Felice. She and her father had been getting along so well. He even seemed to like Kevin in spite of himself. But after this, all of the good will that had been built up between them would go down the tubes.

"Hi, little girl." Richard LeCroix greeted Felice as she walked into the door. There were still a few customers leisurely enjoying a long lunch in the small restaurant. The tables were round with plastic checkered tablecloths, adorned with two long candles each.

"Hi, Uncle." She approached him and kissed him absently on the cheek. "Is Dad around?"

"Sure. He's in the office." Richard smiled at his niece. "What causes you to grace us with your illustrious presence?"

She shot him a look. "Give me a break. I've been up to my ears in Creole food since forever. I'm a little worn out."

"Yeah, I know. Jean is a not-so-frequent visitor here, too." Jean was Richard's twenty-four-year-old son.

"Well, there you go."

"But the problem is I don't get to see you that much," he said as he put his arm around her shoulders. Richard had no daughters and had always spoiled Felice, who was his oldest niece.

"I know. School is taking up most of my time."

"I bet. And I bet that boyfriend of yours is taking up the rest of your time. Oh, I almost forgot! Your father has a visitor in the back office. And, if I'm not mistaken, it's that boyfriend that's taking up so much of his time."

Felice turned to look at her uncle. "Tall, about six-five, brown hair, blue eyes?"

"That's him. Looks to be about twenty-one or twenty-two. Got a little bit of gray in his hair."

"That's him! How long has he been in there?"

"About fifteen minutes. What's wrong, girl?"

"Nothing!" Felice rushed toward the office. What would Kevin be doing here to see her father? Suddenly, she knew. Kevin was going to tell Joseph what had happened this weekend. She had to get in there before Kevin spilled the beans.

She knocked on the door. "Come in," was her father's breezy reply.

She opened the door to her father's and Kevin's smiling faces. Joseph was sitting behind the cluttered desk and Kevin was sitting in a chair on the side of the desk. On the walls were pictures from bygone era and some more recent ones. Felice glanced at the colorized photo of Jean

Tomas LeCroix, her late grandfather. His caramel-colored face seemed to smile knowingly at her.

Her attention turned back to the two living men in front of her. So different, but maybe it only seemed to be so. Both were tall, stolid, and fearless. Both were open, honest, and funny. And both of them loved her.

Joseph was the first to speak. "Hi, baby. Fancy meeting you here."

"Uh, hi Daddy....hi Kevin," she gulped.

"Hi, darl...Felice."

Joseph looked at the younger man with some amusement. "It's okay if you call her 'darling' in my presence, kid. Just don't get too out of hand."

Kevin grinned a bit nervously at him. "No, sir."

Felice observed this banter with total confusion. Suddenly impatience took over. "So, are either of you two going to tell me what's going on here?"

"What's going here," Kevin said as he stood up, "is that I wanted to talk to your dad for a bit. We had a nice chat, and now I gotta go work out." He strode over to her and kissed her on the forehead. "See you tomorrow, same time as usual?"

"Okay." He grinned at her puzzled look, turned to wink at Joseph and walked out.

Felice turned to her father. "What was that about, Dad? Come on, tell me."

"In a minute. You obviously came here to tell me something specific. Why else would you be in the restaurant. You've acted like this place has cooties for a while now."

"Come on, Dad." She sat in the chair that Kevin had vacated. "You know I'm real busy with school."

"Okay, baby. Now what did you want to tell me?"

She took a deep breath. Then she told him the whole story of Kevin's visit to her hotel room in Santa Fe and its outcome.

"I will admit, Daddy, that the thought had crossed both our minds to...you know...but I didn't want to. I wasn't ready and to tell the truth, I don't think he was, either." She sat forward and spoke urgently to her father. "He understood what I was feeling and was a perfect gentleman about everything and I do mean everything. He didn't try to change my mind or talk me into it."

Joseph's face was unreadable. "So, why didn't you want to..." The words seemed to be stuck on the tip of his tongue. It was the first time he had ever talked about sex with his daughter. "...make love?"

"Because...it didn't seem right to...give a part of yourself to someone without...being committed to him."

Joseph was quiet. Felice looked at him with some alarm. "Please, Daddy. Don't be angry with him," she pleaded. "Be angry with me. I knew that he was going to visit. I tried to talk him out of it, but not hard enough. Don't take my mistake out on him."

"I won't take it out on him. And yes, you didn't try hard enough. What did Kevin say that you told him? 'Please don't make me into a liar.'"

Felice was speechless. Joseph went on.

"He took responsibility for the whole thing. I'd say that *both* of you are responsible."

Felice sat stunned, looking miserably at him.

"I'm sorry, Daddy."

Joseph looked at his daughter sternly and then his face softened. "Apology accepted. The only reason that I'm accepting it is that the two of you came to me, independently from the looks of it, to tell me the truth. I have to respect both of you for that. To be honest, Felice, I'm actually very proud of you for it, very proud." He leaned over and kissed her gently on the forehead.

She smiled at him uncertainly. "Are you going to punish me for this?"

Joseph shrugged his shoulders and grinned at her slyly. "It'd be kind of pointless to forbid you to have anything to do with Kevin. You see each other all the time at school and I think that it would be overreacting a bit if I got a restraining order on him or a bodyguard for you."

"Daddy!"

"Calm down. Can't your old dad have a little fun dreamin'? Besides, in spite of this incident, or perhaps because of it, I think Kevin's a fine young man. I was wrong about him."

Felice was speechless again as Joseph went on.

"It's wrong to judge a person's character because that person looks like someone who hurt you. I had to work through my prejudice, knowing it was wrong, but feeling it anyway. Your mother says it's a test from God and I'm inclined to believe that. I hope I've passed. I'd say you've passed too, little girl."

"I'm not a little girl anymore, Daddy," she said with amusement.

"Boy, don't I know that! But cut me some slack. I'll probably call you that when you're forty.

"Kevin and I sat here and talked about...quite a few things before your arrival. I learned a lot about him in a short time. He told me a little about his mother, about how it's just been him and his father for quite some time. He told me about you and how you fit into his life."

"What'd he say?"

"Now, you know I'm not going to tell you everything, girl. But I'd say the man cares a great deal about you. And why shouldn't he? You're a lovely young lady, sweetheart."

Felice smiled shyly at him.

"He also said that his father likes you, which, according to him, isn't always a given with everyone he meets."

"I like him, too. He's a nice man, very easy to be around."

Joseph smiled enigmatically at his daughter. "I know. He's real. Just like his son.

****

It was eleven-fifteen A.M., a day later. Felice walked expectantly along the perimeter of the cafeteria inside the Quad. Kevin was usually waiting for her in the Quad at a table on the outside edge of the cafeteria part of the building. Magically, he always was able to secure an empty table every day, though the Quad was always packed with people at that time of day. But without him, getting a table was next to impossible. *Guess thems the perks when you're the Big Cheesehead,* she thought sardonically. She made a mental note to call him that later on.

It was unheard of, in her experience for Kevin to be late without, somehow, letting her know beforehand. By eleven forty-five, she gave up, very worried. Where could he be?

She walked out of the Quad and nearly bumped into Kevin.

"What happened? I was worried about you."

"Nothing. I had to take care of something. Come on. Let's go back in the Quad."

"But I've got to go to class...."

"It'll be okay. You'll get to class soon enough. Come on. I've got something to show you. You're gonna like it...I hope." He led her to the semi-circled, high-backed seat where he had first spoken to her. Sitting there were five, tuxedo-clad football players, including Malik Hayes. In unison, they all got up, cleared their throats and began to sing.

The first song was "Let Me Call You Sweetheart," sung surprisingly well. Felice laughed delightedly at Malik's antics and clapped appreciatively along with the growing crowd.

The next song was "Let's Stay Together" with Malik singing lead in a clear tenor and his back-up singers doing a hilarious impression of the Temptations.

After the crowd again showed its appreciation, Malik walked up to Felice, took her hand, and walked over to Kevin and took his hand.

"Felice, I think Kevin has something he wants to say to you." Then Malik stepped back. The crowd fell into an unnaturally, hushed silence.

Kevin took both of Felice's hands into his. "Felice, I just want to tell you right here in front of God and everybody, that you are the best thing that's ever happened to me. You're beautiful, smart, generous, sweet, and wonderful and I wanted everyone to know that that's what I think about you. I want everyone to know that I love you."

Felice's mouth almost wouldn't work. She felt tears welling up. "I think all those things about you, too, baby, and more," she said in a near whisper. "And I love you."

"Well since that's the situation, there's only one thing to do."

He got down on one knee as the crowd let out a whooping cheer, and stretched out his hand to Malik. Malik fished a ring box out of his jacket pocket and handed it to him. Then the crowd quieted down to hear him and to hear her answer.

"Will you marry me?'

She caught her breath and looked at him.

"Are you crazy?" she shouted. "Of course, I'll marry you!"

He got up and lifted her off the floor, kissing her hard as the crowd clapped and cheered and whistled.

* * *

The informal meeting would come to order in Trevor's dorm room in nearly an hour. Usually when the fraternity brothers had a meeting, the format was scheduled and filled with ritual. But this meeting was only for a selected few of the members: five members whom Trevor trusted to keep their mouths shut about the act of retribution that Trevor wanted to exact. Oh, sure, all the Taus were commanded to keep any secret that a big brother command them to. However, the action that Trevor wanted to execute was no ordinary action. This type of thing was only for his most trustworthy lieutenants.

They had carried out such doings in the past. The most recent one had been against Adrienne Anderson, but it had been foiled by that ho, Felice. Felice. She always seemed to be a fly in every ointment. At first, Trevor had thought she was just some timid airhead with a nice backside. He had gotten himself a piece, passed her on to one of his minions, and had given her no more thought.

But on the afternoon that they had tried to teach Adrienne a lesson, Felice had been like a lioness. Trevor had privately been impressed. He had thought she was some silly, little girl with loose knees, but he had been wrong. She was far more dangerous than any of them had given her credit for, and far more resilient. After Trevor and the other Taus had pulled Daniel's coat about Felice's prior extracurricular activities, and Daniel had promptly dumped her, Trevor had often seen Felice walking around campus alone looking as though she were about to cry at any moment. The other brothers had seen her as well, and they

all had congratulated themselves on a job well done. Trevor
supposed he felt some sympathy for her but he had quickly
pushed that aside. She had interfered with Tau justice—
interfered in the black Man's business. He supposed that
they could have taken both women down, but that would
have just been too risky. And the revenge that they *had*
taken had been so much more effective, or so he had
thought at the time.

But the little skank was like a weeble: she wobbled,
but she kept getting back up. She goes out and gets a *white
boy*! And not just any old white boy, but the biggest, most
popular devil on campus. Then she had the nerve to bring
him to the A.C.C dinner. Oh they had tried to corral him,
but he had made them look like fools.   It was all *her* fault for
bringing him in the first place. She had, once again, over-
stepped her bounds; *she just did not get it.*

Then, there was that big spectacle in the Quad
the other day. So, the white idiot wanted to marry the little
slut, did he? What kind of crap was that? And that hoochie
Felice had said yes. Yes, she was far more dangerous than
he had thought. She was a traitor to her own race.

Oh sure, he and some of his frat brothers played
around with white girls, but most would never think about

marrying one. How would that look if they wanted to hold themselves up as champions of the race? How would that look when the time for vengeance, retribution, and redistribution came?

So, the big football idiot thought he could do or say anything he wanted to the great Taus. Well, he was about to find out that he couldn't. Trevor found himself happy that football season was over. That devil might find himself too banged up to throw a pass and Trevor certainly didn't want to be responsible for messing up the Tigers chances for a national championship. *No. We couldn't have that,* he grinned to himself.

"Okay, now what we need is for someone to trail Hart three times next week to see what his general pattern is. Actually, we need three someone's, so he won't get suspicious."

Trevor paused expectantly, waiting for volunteers. In four seconds, he got them.

"Okay we got 'Dre on Monday, Jamal on Wednesday, and Tommy on Friday, so no one person will miss too much class. Any suggestions?"

"I think we ought to keep an eye out for Felice," said Jamal. "She'll recognize us even if the white boy doesn't."

"I couldn't care less about that back-stabbing bitch," spat Andre Carter.

"I don't think any of us do either 'Dre, but I'm betting Jamal's point was that Felice could recognize one of us and alert her massa to what might be going on," said Trevor.

"That's it exactly, Big Brother," said Jamal.

"Okay," Trevor went on. "If Felice is with him, we'll cease and desist, but if he's alone, we follow him. After we establish his pattern, we'll meet here, same time, on Monday, the week after the surveillance. Then we'll decide where the action will take place."

Chapter Twelve

Felice sat in the campus library pouring over her political science notes, once, twice, then a third time. She had banished all thoughts of Kevin from her mind, though it had been difficult. Four months prior, she had felt as though everything had been closing around her. What a difference a semester made.

The final for this class was at the end of the week. She had already taken the other three and was sure that she had done 'A' work, not that it mattered officially. The other classes were repeats of failures, so she would only receive a 'C' in each. However, she could receive an actual 'A' in this one, so she was making every effort to ensure that this would happen. She was feeling pretty proud of herself.

Felice looked at her watch. It was ten o'clock! How had she lost such track of time? It was her fault for turning the watch's beeper off. The library stayed open until twelve during the two weeks of the finals, but she had been here since six. An 'A' was pretty much in the bag.

However, more immediate matters were on her mind. Her parents would be furious that she hadn't called them to let them know that she would be home late. And it was dark outside. NMU's campus was well-patrolled by security guards, especially at night, but, nevertheless, a couple of rapes and a mugging had occurred within the last few years. At least it wasn't like some of the big city campuses, where assaults on students were the rule, rather than the exception. However, there was one particularly secluded area that she would have to go through. It was the shortest route to the parking lot, and it was also a great place for a rapist or a mugger to lie in wait.

Felice quickly organized her papers and her books and stuffed them into her backpack, mentally chiding herself for not parking closer to the library. She said a quick good-bye to the student-librarian at the desk and headed out of the library door. Stopping for a second on the steps, she did a quick scan of the surrounding area, mentally planning her route to her car. Just as she stepped onto the walkway, she noticed a tall, dark and familiar figure out of the corner of her eye, coming out of the library. She turned around.

"Malik! Thank goodness. I didn't see you in the library."

"Yes, I know. Fine women are always glad to see me," he grinned. "Besides, us jocks gotta hit the books for finals, too. What you doin' out so late, girl? Kevin's gonna whip your behind for worryin' him."

"I *don't* think so."

"Okay, so he won't. But I bet your parents will."

"Uh.....maybe. Anyway I'm glad to see you. You can walk me to my car, pretty please?"

"Oh, I love it when women beg." She playfully pushed him.

"Sir Malik Hayes at your service. Always happy to assist a damsel in distress." He gave her a courtly bow.

They walked in friendly silence for a few seconds. It was a beautiful, cool, clear night, contrasting the relentless June heat of the day. Felice was just beginning to think of Albuquerque as her home. She looked up at the sky, marveling at the myriad stars. This was one of the many advantages, she was discovering, to living here. She had never seen so many stars when living in L.A. She turned and looked at Malik. He seemed to also be enjoying the desert climate.

"Sure isn't like L.A. here, is it, little girl?

"Nor like Detroit, I imagine."

"Hell no. In Detroit, you'd have to wear a flak jacket to school."

"In L.A., you'd wear one of those, too, along with a gas mask."

"So, you and White Lightnin' are gonna take the plunge, eh?"

"Yep." She smiled in wonder that it was really going to happen. "I guess we'll invite you."

"You better get with the program, girl. *I* am the best man. I might even push your pops out the way and give away the bride."

"Yeah, okay. Daddy was a defensive back in college. He might have slowed down a step or two since then, but I bet he could probably still give a good hit or two to some scrawny little receiver like you, given a good reason."

"Maybe so, but he's gotta catch me first. Anyway, there's gonna be a whole lotta white girls cryin' on that day."

"Hey, that's not my problem. They had their chance."

"A few brothas'll be cryin', too."

"I doubt that."

"Sure they will." He grinned playfully at her. "Like me, for instance. You know if Kev wasn't my boy, I'da taken you away from him by now."

"Nah. It would have been too much like incest."

"Now I *know* I'm slippin' when a fine woman thinks of me as her brother! Are you going to invite Mandy?"

"Why not? She's chilled out a lot. I had a great time when the four of us went out. I guess you two have become pretty good friends." She grinned at him.

"I guess." Malik paused for a second then grew serious.

"Felice-change of subject. I have to tell you something and you're not going to like it."

"Please don't confess your undying love for me, Malik. It might complicate the wedding a little."

"I'm the one who told Kevin about your...reputation. It was before I knew you and found out how cool you were." Malik began to speak quickly and desperately. "You and

Kevin didn't even know each other then! I had heard it from some of them tired Taus. I didn't mean any harm! I..."

"Malik, Malik! Stop. I already knew this."

His eyes widened. "You did?"

"Well, I didn't know for sure, but I could figure it out. When I used to see you in the African Cultural Center, you'd be with them...."

"Not *with* them."

"Okay, talking to them sometimes. I put two and two together."

"So...how come you've always been so nice to me?"

She looked over at him solemnly but confidently. The words, which had been rolling around in her head for some months now, flowed easily.

"Let me explain something to you. What I did, I did because I made bad decisions. No one put a gun to my head and made those decisions for me. My parents have told me for years that when a person does something, good or bad, that person has to live with the consequences of whatever they did, whether they're good consequences or bad ones. I didn't really listen when they were telling me this. I had to knock my head against a brick wall to learn that lesson. My bad decisions resulted in me gaining a reputation as a 'ho.'

My good decisions resulted in me staying in school in spite of that and gaining Kevin as my fiancé and you as my friend."

"Oh." Malik thought for a second. "Hold up! A minute ago I was your brother!"

"You're that, too." She grabbed his arm and stood on tip-toes to give him a peck on the cheek. Malik's caramel-colored face reddened slightly.

"You better stop that," he said with slanted grin. "Folks might see you kiss me and start sayin' that you going to be practicin' a little double husbandry."

She burst out laughing. "Screw folks.'"

"Watch your mouth, girl! Who's gonna be your maid of honor? Is it gonna be that big, fine Adrienne? She can wrap those dreads around me anytime! Hmm, I can't wait!"

"I'm going to tell Mandy what you just said."

"No...no please?"

Felice laughed. They continued on their way, with Malik chattering his usual stream of comedy, punctuated by Felice's laughter.

The secluded area that Felice had feared walking through, a small cul-de-sac bordering the parking structure, was about a hundred feet away, but it seemed that several people were in there. Both Felice and Malik stopped talking because they had heard a familiar voice. They rounded the corner in time to see Kevin surrounded by five men. One was about five feet away from Kevin and pointing a gun directly at his head. Malik was immediately on the dead run just as the gun went off.

Chapter Thirteen

Kevin was heading toward the parking lot, his mind swirling with all of what had become his life, his wonderful life. He was finally graduating with a degree in business. He was going to marry a beautiful, intelligent woman whom he loved and who loved him. And to top it off, he had a career that he loved and would get rich on.

The representatives of several NFL teams pursued him relentlessly, pressuring him to make that final decision. Which team would he choose? So many offers to choose from; how could anyone possibly choose?

He would meet tomorrow for dinner with a representative for the New Orleans Saints. As always, his father would accompany them. *Boy, was it nice to have a father who was a lawyer*, Kevin thought. *It takes a shark to know a shark.* Herbert's soft, easy manner hid his steely determination. The word was out now among NFL scouts and sports agents. When dealing with Kevin Hart, watch out for the Old Man.

What had he done for his life to be so wonderful? He had a beautiful fiancée that he loved *and* liked. He looked forward to having a job that he loved doing. One of his father's friends, an Air Force fighter pilot, had told him when he was a boy, that the only jobs worth having were rock-and-roll star, movie star, professional athlete or an Air Force fighter pilot. "Or a lawyer," his father had added hopefully. Well, he had one of those jobs.

Kevin didn't know what he might do after football. All he knew is that God had given him the best life in the world and that he would do his best to make the most of it.

With his head spinning with his great good fortune, he paid no attention as he walked into the false cul-de-sac that led into the parking structure. Hearing the murmuring of several deep voices, he looked up. There were five black men standing in front of him. He recognized a couple of them. They were from that Tau Sigma Pi fraternity, a black fraternity. He remembered a couple of them from the dinner. Some of them had been the ones who had forced him out of the back door of the dinner hall and tried to tell him why he shouldn't have been at the dinner with Felice. He fractionally relaxed. These guys were students. They might want to do a little intimidation but no real harm. Then he remembered what Felice had told him about their confrontation with Adrienne.

Kevin steeled himself, and then nodded his head in greeting at a couple of them. He got no response, but it seemed as though they would let him pass. Then one moved to block his progress.

"Hey, ain't you that white punk that likes himself a little black pussy?" sneered a voice behind him.

"Well he sure don't like it fresh, because that one's been used a bunch of times," said another at his back. "Ain't that damn good, either. I guess you white boys like fourth-hand goods."

Kevin turned around to look at the four behind him. "Nice to see you fellas again. In my experience, a woman is only as good as the man she's with," he said, remembering his father's words to him. "If she's got one who knows what he's doing and who cares about her, she'll be the best thing a man's ever had. Guess you guys didn't know which buttons to push." Kevin smirked. "A woman's got three buttons. I will do y'all a favor, not that you deserve it, but I will. I'll tell you where the two main buttons on a woman are. They're here and here." He pointed at his head and his chest. "Once you realize what's going on in those two places, that third button is a cinch. You guys must not be too bright. A couple of you had a brilliant and beautiful woman with a good heart and you used her for a mattress tag. Just because you didn't realize what you had, don't blame me."

Kevin turned back to the man blocking his way. What was his name? Kevin racked his brain; Trevor--one of the ones who had been with Felice. "So, what now?" He said to the man, obviously the leader.

"What happens now is this," said Trevor. "Apparently, you don't understand talk, so we *make* you understand that you have no right to disrespect black men in public, nor do you have the right to take our women for yourself."

Kevin was astounded. "*Your* women? You treat her like crap, turn her name to mud all over this campus, but now all of a sudden she's *yours*? Correct me if I'm wrong, but didn't they outlaw slavery in this country about one hundred thirty years ago?

"Do not take your ancestors' dirty deeds and twist them to suit your own purposes. We are not like you!" Trevor's teeth were clenched. "Even if none of us want her, she should be with an appropriate man-a *black* man."

"Yeah, she tried that, but you screwed that up for her, too. I know all about it."

"It would be better for her to be alone for the rest of her life than with one of the children of slave-owners."

"So now you, someone who doesn't give one damn about her, are going to decide how she should run her life. Sounds like slavery to me."

Kevin felt the wind of swift movement and heard the unmistakable 'click' of a cocked revolver behind him. He whirled around. The first man that had spoken to him was holding a gun pointed directly at his head.

"Didn't my big brother tell you?" yelled the man. "Do *not* twist our words or our actions and make us like you! *You* are the devil, the white enemy! *You* are the one that deserves to die!"

Kevin looked at the man's eyes, then at his gun. Here was a factor he had never considered when he first noticed the fraternity brothers, nor at anytime during their conversation. They were going to kill him. They had planned it, laid in wait and now, they were ready to execute their plan and him. Kevin decided that he wasn't afraid. His life had been short, but it had been everything that anyone could ask for.   He found himself thinking of God and became calm.

In his unruffled state, he was able to take his eyes off of the man with the gun and look at the other three men in front of him. He now saw clearly that the plan hadn't been to kill him, for all three had expressions of shock and fear on their faces.

"Don't do it, man," said one. "They'll put us all in jail forever! This one isn't the one! Let him have Felice if he wants!"

"'Dre," said a stunned and trembling voice behind Kevin. "Little Brother, this isn't what we wanted. We want to teach him a lesson, make him understand, but not kill him. He can't understand if he's dead." Trevor stepped out from behind Kevin and approached the gunman. "You're right, Little Brother," he said. "We are not like him or his kind. We may debate, demand, or even explain with force, but we aren't murderers." His voice was soft and pleading. To Kevin, he seemed to almost be in tears. Trevor stopped at the gunman's side.

"Little Brother, I love you. I don't want to see you go to prison or get a death sentence." Trevor was almost whispering into the man's ear. "There are far too many of us there already. Think, Little Brother." Andre began to lower the weapon.

Then Kevin, in his fearless state, made a mistake. He spoke to the man.

"If you kill me, you won't hurt me. You'll hurt the people that love me, yes; my father and my girl. But, the person you'll hurt the most is yourself."

"Shut up, white punk!" Andre raised the weapon again. "I don't care about your devil-father or your race-traitor bitch! It will be worth it to go to prison if I can send you to Hell!" Then, just as Trevor grabbed his shooting arm, he fired.

For an instant, Malik halted in his tracks, his eyes wide with disbelief as he watched his friend fall. Then, he rushed Andre Carter, tackling him with the expertise of his long experience at playing football. The gun went flying, clattering on the concrete. Malik, who hadn't been in a fist fight since his early high school years, got up with Andre Carter's shirt collar in his hand and began to viciously pummel and curse the man as tears streamed down his own face. Andre's fraternity brothers made no move to assist their comrade.

Felice's backpack lay on the ground behind her. When the gun had been fired, it seemed as though all time had stopped for her. She stood, unmoving, in one spot as if rooted there. She had turned to stone.

She was only dimly aware of the commotion around her. Her eyes were fixed on Kevin, his long body lying prone on the concrete with a pool of blood spreading beneath it.

Chapter Fourteen

Tom Wade's mind was on automatic as he patrolled the first floor of Parking Structure A. His wife would probably have chicken made, ready for him to microwave as soon as he got home after his shift ended at twelve. He hated working the late shift, mostly because it was so boring. There was no one to talk to, no students hustling their way to class, no pretty, young girls to ogle. The few cars that were still there would likely be there for the night.

However, this state of events would change in the summer session. Tom had managed to trade shifts with a young single, guy. He would be able to spend more time with his family, be there when his son got home from school, be there to eat dinner with his wife, be there to check out the TV shows they were always talking about, and be there for Monday Night Football.

But, most of all, he could have a little excitement at work. It was June and the coeds were wearing their shorts, halters, and mini-skirts. A little visual stimulation never hurt anyone.

He looked at his watch. It was ten-ten P.M. Another hour and fifty minutes left on his shift, just four more boring patrols around the structure and he'd be done. As he passed the west exit, he thought he heard soft murmuring. Slightly tense, he glanced through the egress, but in the darkness, he could see no one, nor detect any movement. *You ain't but thirty-five*, he chuckled to himself. You're way too young to be imagining things.

He headed toward the stairs to patrol the second floor. Just as he made it to the top of the first flight of stairs, the deafening, unmistakable sound of a high-caliber weapon assaulted his infantry-trained ears. He whirled around, nearly leaping to the bottom of the stairs. Then he remembered that he wasn't carrying a firearm. None of the campus security did. At a campus in a relatively crime-free city, the security management hadn't deemed it necessary. *A lot they knew,* thought Tom as he slowed to prowl by stealth. He inched his way up to the entrance, as his infantry training kicked in like an old, forgotten instinct. Suddenly, on this, relatively cool night, he was drenched with sweat. He hoped that whoever it was wouldn't be able to smell him. There was a trash can close to the exit that he could use for cover. This was one of the few times that he was happy to be a short, slight man. He could fit his body easily behind the trash can in the parking structure and slip out to hide behind the one that was right outside the building. Crawling on the ground, as he had done in the verdance of Germany's Black Forest and of Grenada, he made his way outside.

As his eyes adjusted to the darkness, he began to make out the forms of five people. Blacks. No wonder he hadn't been able to see them when he had looked out the doorway.

Niggers always mean trouble, he thought as he tried to see more. After the army, he had moved his family to Albuquerque, a city that didn't have too many niggers. A situation like this was proof that it only took a few of them to cause trouble.

Tom was beginning to be able to make out more details. One of them was a woman. She appeared to be just standing there. She was standing so still that, if Tom hadn't known the layout of the campus so well, he would have thought she was one of the statues erected to depict NMU's founders. She seemed to have her attention fixed on something on the ground.

The others were not quite so stationary. Their attention was directed at a commotion between yet two other people. One was beating up another one.

Tom inched his head up a little higher so he could see what the woman was staring at. A jolt rocked through him as he was finally able to discern the entire picture. There was a white kid, a tall one, lying unmoving on the ground.

He managed to inch himself back into the parking structure. He raced up the stairs to the second floor and pulled out his walky-talky.

"Control, this is Guard 4," he said softly, trying to keep the niggers from hearing him and to keep the trembling out of his voice.

"Guard 4, this is Control. Go ahead."

"There's been a shooting outside of the west entrance of Parking Structure A!"

"Control to Guard 4, please repeat."

"I said there's been a shooting outside the west entrance of parking structure A. We need an ambulance and the police over here! There's a man lying on the ground surrounded by a gang of folks. The victim is a white male. It looks a little bit like Kevin Hart. There's a gang of n.... black people around him. They did it!

"Ten-four!"

Tom let go of the send button on the walky-talky and sat down on the top step to wait for the sound of the sirens. *Damn niggers,* he thought. *That's what they get for letting them in a good school like this one.*

Her mind...what mind? How could wit, intellect, knowledge of history, literature, and science stop this? How could her education, her doing well in school, her understanding of logic and foreign languages stop this? How could her love for her family and friends stop this? How could her love for Kevin stop this? Her mind was useless to her. She felt it beginning to shut off.

It was only when she saw Kevin's head move that she realized that the spreading pool of blood was beneath his legs.

"Felice."

Her paralysis was broken and she ran over to him.

"I'm here, hon." She looked around to see, almost for the first time, that the fraternity brothers hadn't fled and that Malik was beating the daylights out of one of them. It barely registered on her that it was Andre Carter.

"Malik! Kevin's alive! Call an ambulance!" She saw Malik stand up. As he turned to her, he let Andre's unconscious form drop to the ground. He kicked it and then ran over to them. Felice noticed that his face was wet.

"Don't worry, brother," he said to Kevin, as he bent down opposite from Felice. "Somebody must have heard the shot because I hear an ambulance."

A lone siren could be heard in the distance, but Felice thought she heard multiple car engines much closer. Then the sound ceased. There were slammings of doors and the poundings of large, running feet against concrete. Then, almost inevitably, there were the clicking sounds of multiple gun bolts being cocked.

"Freeze, all of you! Police. All hands where we can see them!"

Felice looked around perplexed. Did they mean her? She didn't want to leave Kevin. Then, suddenly, she had no choice.

"Get up! What? You think you're too cute to get shot?" Felice turned toward the sneering male voice and came face-to-face with the barrel of a .44. In disbelief, she slowly stood up, raising her hands in the air, just like she had seen TV criminals do. They actually thought she had something to do with shooting Kevin!

The ambulance, after destroying much of NMU's landscape in that area, screeched to halt, as the emergency medical technicians nearly simultaneously jumped out and ran to the rear of the vehicle. Within a few seconds, they were at Kevin's side. Felice could hear them as they quickly went through their 'ABCs,' which she vaguely remembered from a CPR course she had taken in high school. *Please God,* she prayed. *Don't let him bleed to death.*

The police had made Malik get up from Kevin's side as well. About twelve police officers had surrounded the entire group, herding them into a frightened pack. Handcuffs were placed on every one of them, including Felice and a waking Andre Carter, who was in no shape to resist. Felice looked at the policewoman who placed her hands behind her back.

"We didn't do anything," she pleaded with the woman, as she inclined her head toward Malik.

"He didn't do anything! The one with the green shirt...he's Kevin's friend and I'm Kevin's fiancée. We were trying to save him from the others." The woman was about to give her a sarcastic, disbelieving response, when one of the EMTs breathlessly approached them.

"Excuse me officer, but the patient is calling for a Felice LeCroix. He says she's out here and that she's his fiancée."

"I'm Felice LeCroix." The officer looked at her. Still, disbelief filled her face.

"Do you have some ID?"

"Yes. It's in my backpack over there." She gestured again with her head.

The woman seemed to take her time getting to the pack. Felice was frantic. The EMT gave her a sympathetic look.

"Will you get it out, already?" The EMT shouted. "He's bleeding to death. We've got to get him outta here!" The woman reached into the pack and slowly took out the wallet. Felice's driver's license was right in front.

"Felice," the woman read slowly. "Le... it's too dark. I can't see this face." Her voice was sardonic. She walked up to another officer. "Can you see this face? Think that's her?"

Before the other officer could reply, the EMT had located the sergeant of the group.

"Sergeant, one of your officers is endangering the life of the patient! Did you recognize the patient at all? It's Kevin Hart and he's calling for a Felice LeCroix, the woman that you guys have under arrest. Your officer seems to not want to let her go. She says her name is Felice LeCroix and your officer has her ID. I don't know what your officer's problem is, but I do know this: if he bleeds to death, I'll make sure that everyone in New Mexico knows why!"

The sergeant sprang immediately to action. "Williams," he shouted at the policewoman. "What's the hold up? Let me see that ID!" He trotted over to her, literally snatched the license from her hand and trained his flashlight on it. "It's her. Get the cuffs off her so she can go with the ambulance. Now!"

The woman took the cuffs off and Felice ran to the back of the ambulance. One of the EMTs tending to Kevin stuck out his hand and helped her in. Within less than a minute, siren blaring, the ambulance was on its way.

"I keep telling you I had nothing to do with this. The man that got shot was my friend." Malik sat being questioned in an interrogation room in the APD precinct closest to NMU. He had insisted on his innocence throughout the entire trip there and when that had no effect, he had begun insulting the officers, questioning their intelligence. By the time the group had arrived at the precinct, all of the officers were tired of him. In lock-up, they had isolated him from the Taus, and now, one of the officers questioned him alone.

"Don't try to get out of this," the officer now said. "Your friends all said that you were with them," he lied.

"Then they're lying and they are not my friends," Malik said vehemently. "They are the ones who ganged up on Kevin and they shot him. My other friend, Felice, the girl that went with the ambulance, and I had just walked up when they shot him."

The officer hunched down directly in Malik's face. "Don't give me that bullshit. All of you ganged up on him, for whatever reason. Maybe just because you found a lone, unprotected white boy, or maybe because he was getting himself some black pussy that you wanted."

Malik had just about had enough. He put his face even closer to that of the man's. "Look. Are you stupid or something?" he sneered. "All you have to do is ask anyone on campus or ask Felice or ask Kevin when he wakes up. I'm his best friend."

"We're asking you, stupid."

"You police." Malik's voice had dropped to a calm and conversational tone. He stared nearly unblinkingly into the man's eyes. "You're all the same, whether it's here or in Detroit. Can't you hear? I told you what happened. All you see is my black face and it blocks your ears. That makes you think I've lied or stolen or tried to kill someone. I've told you the truth. If you can't hear it, that's your problem."

This is going nowhere, thought McDuffy. *This smart-mouthed nigger needs to be convinced that talking is in his best interest.*

McDuffy glared at the suspect for a moment, receiving an equally penetrating gaze in return. Yeah, this one is too smart for his own good. He needs to be shown what he really is.

McDuffy stepped to the door of the room and opened it slightly.

"Walters, come on in," he said softly. The door opened wider as he stepped back. McDuffy watched as Hayes turned around to see what came next. He grinned at the fear that he saw in Hayes' face. Then, after an instant, it was gone. Walters was six feet eight inches and close to three hundred pounds. He watched as Walters bore down on the suspect and reached out to slap him with his massive hand.

"What are you looking at, nigger," the huge police officer roared. "I didn't give you permission to look at me!"

Malik's face felt as if someone had hit him with a boulder. He put his hand to the moistness he suddenly felt trickling from his nose. He looked at his hand. Blood.

The new officer was suddenly opposite of Malik, on the other side of the table. The man picked up the table and hurled it against the wall. Malik started to get up from the chair, but the man was lightening-quick for his size. Malik's shoulders were gripped by two vise-like hands as he was slammed back onto the chair, nearly overturning it.

"Going somewhere? We're not through talking." The man's voice had dropped to a near-whisper. Malik sat as far back in the chair as he could. The man's crotch was just about at the level of his nose.

"So you don't want to cooperate with us. How about if I make you suck my dick? Think that'll make you a little more talkative?" He grinned over McDuffy.

"I've told the other officer everything I know. I swear it's the truth." Malik was struggling to keep the fear out of his voice. Suddenly he heard a voice in his head, one that he thought he recognized. Be strong. Be strong, little brother. It was...Alex. But how could it be? Alex was dead eight years. Murdered. Murdered by...by Detroit police officers. Alex had been a gang member for sure, but on that night he had been doing nothing illegal- just hanging out on the corner with a couple of friends, not a block from his parents' house. The police had just walked up on him and shot him in the back of the head. They claimed he had pointed a gun at them but the witnesses—the ones who refused to talk to the police--had said that he had his hands in his pockets. No arrests were made and the officer who had done the shooting kept his job, and Malik's mother lost her mind.

Malik's fear died away. He looked up at the huge man's eyes. They were brown and nearly opaque. There was not an ounce of hatred in them, not an ounce of anything in them--just the neutral eyes of someone doing his job, what ever that job might entail. His eyes had the impartiality of a corpse. Evil, thought Malik as if in greeting. This is evil; with a bare enough face for anyone to see.

The man lifted Malik up off of the chair by his neck. Malik grabbed at the man's hand, struggling against his superior strength, to no avail. He tried to speak, but his trachea was nearly cut off. Malik tried to break his fall as the man tossed him toward the wall. His slender body crashed against one of the legs of the table that had been tossed there. His legs suddenly began to feel numb. He coughed as breath returned to his body, then he looked up at those dead eyes again.

"Is that the best you can do?" Malik's near breathlessness couldn't hide the sneer in his voice. "Us niggers are a little harder than that. Is the truth too hard for your monkey-mind to grasp? Fine. It's still the truth and it won't change just because you want it to. I told you I had nothing to do with the shooting. Beating the shit out of me won't change it."

The man cocked his head sideways at his quarry, as though a new tactic had suddenly jumped into his head. Malik watched calmly as the man put his hand out to the other officer. The other officer pulled his nightstick off of his own belt.

There was one consuming thought in Malik's head as his consciousness, his life, slipped from his grasp. *All praise due to the Father, Son, and the Holy Spirit. Please let my Daddy get through this, dear Jesus Christ,* prayed Malik as the blows rained down on his head. *Please don't let this break his....*

Chapter Fifteen

Blackness was Kevin's world, at least for the moment. He sensed that there was another world, the one in which he belonged. It was a world that he dreaded reentering, but it was *his* world, nonetheless. He struggled to find that other world, but it seemed as though his mind were trudging through a tar pit. His mind began to tire and he dissolved back into the peaceful blackness.

Kevin's eyes opened wide. He was finally in that world, that terrible, horrible world. It was a world of whiteness; white walls, white sheets: a hospital. For nearly a minute, he had no idea how he had arrived in that place or why he was there. Then, in a flash, he remembered. He had been shot.

He tried to bounce out of the bed, but some heavy burden was weighing him down. His large body rebounded and he banged his head slightly on the headboard.

He pushed the covers off of himself and recognized his millstone as an old acquaintance. From hip to ankle, his left leg was encased in plaster. A frightening thought entered his head, but he immediately pushed it away.

Where's that damned button, he thought. But before he could find it, a nurse was opening the door.

"Hello, Mr. Hart. Glad to see your eyes opened. Do you remember what happened to you?"

"Yes. I was shot. Where are my father and my fiancée?"

"They're right outside. I'll get them for you." The nurse left the room.

In a few seconds, the faces he most wanted to see were coming through the door. Herbert was red-eyed and looked like a man who hadn't slept in days, but when he saw his son's eyes open and directed at him, he smiled wide. Then he approached the bed, sat down, and kissed Kevin on the cheek, something that he hadn't done in years.

"Hi, Son." Herbert's voice was breaking.

"Hi, Dad. Felice?" Felice stood a few feet from the bed. She looked at Herbert, as if asking for permission to come over.

"Come on, honey," said Herbert. He got up and led her by the hand. Felice looked at Kevin as though he would disappear at any moment.

"Come on over here, girl. I don't have all day," Kevin smiled at her. She walked slowly over to the bed, sat on the edge of it and laid her head on his chest, as tears streamed down her face. Kevin curled her unruly hair around fingers of one hand.

Herbert watched them, trying to control his own tears. "I'll leave you two alone for a moment."

"Thanks. Daddy?" Kevin looked at his father, his voice that of small child.

"Yes, Son."

"I love you."

The dam that Herbert had been trying to hold back broke. "I love you, too, boy. You are my entire world." He looked at Felice. "Take all the time you need, little girl. Time is something that can't be wasted. I'll be back in a minute, son."

"Okay, Daddy," said Kevin. Herbert stepped through the door.

"Hey, now," Kevin said softly as he raised her face up. "I'm alive. I'm all right." He kissed her softly on the lips.

"Thank God. When that gun went off, I just knew you were dead. I didn't even notice at first that the bastard had shot you in the leg. When Malik...," her voice broke a bit. "When we walked up, the gun was pointed at your head."

"I saw Trevor grab the guy's arm just before he fired. Before that, Trevor had been trying to talk the guy out of shooting me. So, I guess I owe him my life."

"Don't tell me that. Don't try to make me feel anything but hatred for them," spat Felice through clenched teeth. "If they hadn't ganged up on you in the first place...none of this would have happened!"

"But it's the truth, baby. I'm sure the police want to talk to me and I'll tell them that."

"The police!" Felice sneered. Kevin saw another blaze of hatred in her eyes, one which seemed not to be directed at the Taus.

"Don't look like that," Kevin said softly. "You're messing up a pretty face."

"Kevin..." She was holding something back, something terrible.

"Football. I won't be able to play anymore, will I?"

Felice sighed. "According to the doctors, they don't know. But...they doubt it. Your thigh bone was hit. You're going to be in that cast for a while and after they take it off, there's going to be some physical therapy. At least that's what they told your dad." She paused. "There's..."

Kevin put his head back on the pillow. "I guess I figured that out once I woke up and saw that thing on my leg. But I didn't want to admit it to myself." He sighed. *What now?*

"I guess Malik really will be paying for everything," he went on. "Is he outside? Go get him for me, would you?" At Felice's silence, he lifted up his head and looked searchingly at her face. There was something more, something much worse, but he couldn't fathom what it might be. What could be worse than his not being able to play football anymore?

"Felice, what's wrong? Is there something else you need to tell me?"

"Malik's dead, Kevin," she whispered, the tears starting to stream anew. "They killed him," she sobbed.

"What...what are you talking...?" His throat was suddenly as dry as the New Mexico West Mesa. It seemed that his mouth no longer was able to work. "How...the Taus killed...how could they have...?"

"The *police* killed him, Kevin," she poured out. "Just as we walked up on you and the Taus, Carter shot you. Malik rushed him and beat him senseless." Her face was puffy and gray. "But when the police came, they took him into custody with the Taus." Her voice had a tinge of madness to it. "I told them that we had nothing to do with the shooting, but they took him anyway. All they saw was a bunch of black people surrounding a shot white guy. They were going to take me, too. But you called out my name and made the ambulance guys come get me before you passed out."

"What happened? Why did they...how could they have...tell me!" He was hysterical.

"They beat him to death! Beat him for being black. Beat him for hating cops. Beat him for being your friend...they..."

Felice broke off as she put her head back down on Kevin's chest, her sobs filling the sterile room. Kevin made no sound, however. He simply put his head back and closed his twenty-two year old eyes, as his tears began their course down his suddenly ancient face.

* * *

The memorial service was held a week later at Tiger stadium. The 25,000-seat facility had been jam-packed, with thousands standing vigil in the parking lot. It seemed as if the entire city and half of the state came out to mourn the death of Malik Hayes. It also seemed as though the other half of the state were picketing police stations all around Albuquerque. The sense of grief, shock, and anger had nearly overwhelmed the small city. Kevin was still in the hospital and Felice was nearly constantly by his bedside; the hospital staff had wheeled a big-screen TV into the private room so they could see the enormous tribute being paid to their friend. They stared mutely at the screen as the camera caught a pale, drawn, red-eyed Amanda Bain. She was holding white roses in her hands.

They also hadn't been able to attend Malik's funeral, which had been held in Detroit. A broken Elijah Hayes, with his private plane fare having been paid for by the city, had come to collect his son's body a few days after the murder. The adult LeCroix's, Herbert Hart, NMU's president, the mayor of Albuquerque, and the governor of New Mexico had met him at the airport. The president approached him.

"Mr. Hayes, I would like to present you with your son's Bachelor of Science degree in Mathematics. He graduated magna cum laude and has been added to our list of alumni."

"Thank you, sir," whispered Elijah.

"And on behalf of the staff and faculty of NMU, the city and, indeed, the entire state...we can't know what you're feeling..." said the president, uncertainly and with a breaking voice. The man paused. "But, we share in your grief. Your son was greatly loved."

Elijah glared at the man, seeming to be ready to explode. "You're right. You can't possibly know what I'm feeling," he said, full-voiced and matter-of-factly. Then the blinding rage seemed to subside. "But thank you for my son's degree."

Elijah turned to the other part of his greeting party, as if he were going to speak to them. But he merely nodded his head in Herbert Hart's direction and, in a few minutes, reboarded the plane.

The New Mexico University chapter of the Tau Sigma Pi fraternity, along with its sister sorority, was banned from the NMU campus. All the members of the fraternity who had been involved in the incident were expelled. The African Student Union launched a protest against the banning, but they received little support from anyone, even many of its own members.

Andre Carter received twenty years to life in the notoriously brutal New Mexico State Penitentiary in Santa Fe for attempted murder. The jury barely deliberated. The four other men involved in the incident had also been charged with conspiracy to commit attempted murder, but the charges were dismissed, mostly due to Kevin Hart, who, true to his word, had testified that only Andre Carter had known about the gun. None of the four had been from New Mexico and within a day of the dismissal, in anticipation of being ridden out of the state on a rail, all of them were on airplanes back to their various hometowns.

McDuffy and Walters, the two police officers involved in the murder of Malik Hayes, were convicted of aggravated second-degree murder. They would be keeping company with Andre Carter.

"You can go now. You've done your part."

"What? What are you talking about? Is this because the therapy session didn't go so well? It's only the first one. You'll get stronger as you go along."

After six weeks, the well written-on cast had been removed. Kevin looked at his once powerfully-muscled left leg that the surgeons had worked so feverishly to save. It was now nearly as white as the cast had been and, of course, the muscles had begun to atrophy. Right above the knee, there was a thick surgical scar that almost encircled his entire leg, along with an entry wound on the front and the multiple scars of an exit wound on the back.

"Fuck therapy! Is therapy going to bring back my career? I do not give a damn about therapy!"

Felice had expected this, but was shocked, nonetheless. He hardly ever cursed in front of her and never at her.

"I said you can leave now. I'm not the big time athlete anymore. I'm not going to be rolling in millions anymore. So get gone and find another cash man. Now!

Now Felice understood. She stood up, folded her arms, and looked at him.

"Did you hear what I said? Go!" he shouted.

"What are you going to do? Get up and make me leave?"

Kevin tried to get up from the wheelchair but the leg just wouldn't cooperate. He slumped back, turning his head away from her.

"If you want me to go, you're going to have to get your big ass up out of that chair, pick me up and put me out of the door and drop me flat on *my* ass."

"Felice, please just go..."

"You are a moron!" She was shouting at him. Kevin's eyes widened as Felice hotly continued. "You thought that I was only with you because you were a big time athlete? I *never* liked athletes, never! All of you fuckers are idiots! And here you are with all those ugly scars on your shriveled-up leg, talking nonsense and proving my point! It's *you* I love, you big, stupid jock, not your status. God!" She beseeched God with her hands.

"You called me a moron," he said wonderingly.

"So. You going to get up and put me out for that, too? Try it!" She stood with her arms crossed and looked at him challengingly.

"Malik told me that origin of that word once." He smiled in the wake of unexpected nostalgia. "He used it on me once when I kept throwing the ball at his knees." Felice started at Kevin's uttering of Malik's name. Kevin hadn't mentioned their friend at all since Felice had told him that Malik was dead, not even obliquely.

"He said that it referred to an adult with a mental age of between eight and twelve who was capable of doing routine work. He said that he had memorized the definition from Webster's when he was eight." Kevin chuckled at that irony.

Felice's bravado was suddenly gone. "Kevin, you know I didn't mean it that way, so don't try to use it to get me out of here."

"No. I was just startled by the thought of how brilliant he was, how much he knew." He looked at Felice. "You, too. So much for black inferiority."

Kevin stopped talking. He seemed a world away. Suddenly he snapped back to reality.

"Did you know he had an IQ of 160? He showed me his records from an IQ test he took when he was in high school."

"Kevin...," she said gently. "I'll help you get on the bed."

"He didn't like too many people to know how much he knew," he continued as Felice partially supported him getting onto his bed. He had lost a lot of weight, she noticed, about twenty-five pounds. "Said it made him feel like the N who knew too much. He actually said the word out."

She was breathing harder than normal as she sat down next to him. He was still heavy.

"Said it made him feel like a freak. He even wondered about this. Why is it that a smart black person feels so all alone?"

"Well if his IQ was 160, he was smarter than a whole lot of white people, too," she said nonchalantly.

"Definitely smarter than this moron," he said with a sad smile.

"Baby, I'm sorry."

"No, no! *I'm* sorry. I *am* a moron because I don't know jack shit! It was *me* that was supposed to die that night, not him! Me!" His smile was gone and he began to dissolve into tears. "I'm too dumb to know why an idiot like me lives and a smart guy like Malik dies. I don't know a damned thing! If I were smarter, maybe I'd be able to figure out why...."

"Shhh...I love you....shhh..." She put one hand up to wipe his face and that was the last of his self-control. He put his head down on her lap and cried himself to sleep.

In the campus chapel, Felice was alone; courtesy of several of the NMU football and basketball Tigers who had taken it upon themselves to be her bodyguards since the incident. They had even come to the house, met Joseph and Vetra, and of their own volition had basically sworn an oath to the two to keep their daughter safe.

She found herself praying yet again. Praying to It-- praying to the God whose nature she believed that she could not know. She had brought along her mother's Bible, which Vetra had urged her to take when she said where she was going. Somehow, it didn't seem like such an imposition anymore to inform her parents of her whereabouts.

Alone in the chapel, she found herself praying out loud. She didn't know what to pray for so she looked at the large cross in the sanctuary and asked, "God, what do you want me to know and what do you want me to do?" Suddenly, she had the urge to open the bible and it fell open to Matthew 5. She looked down at the page direct at the beginning of the fourth verse at Jesus' words: "Blessed are they that mourn: for they shall be comforted."

Felice found herself in tears again and felt a surge of gratitude—of love—for *Him*, for God. She looked up to the ceiling and said aloud, "My God. Thank you, God, for keeping my Kevin alive."

"Thank you for that wonderful introduction. I'll pay you later for that, Strazinski. My dad, the lawyer, says, 'never underestimate the power of a good bribe.'"

Light laughter came from the seated crowd. It was May 1996 and the sun was high, but not as oppressive as it would be in a month. Kevin looked out on the crowd of dignitaries in front of him. Alumni mostly, like his father, his wife, and himself; some of them great athletes who now played in the NFL, the NBA, and even the NHL.

 He focused his eyes on an enormously pregnant black woman in the front row. She smiled at him. He smiled back.

"My wife says I have a tendency to not know when to shut up, so I'll try not to bore you all into throwing something at me.

"We've all come here to dedicate New Mexico University's new football practice facility to a guy who made Jerry Rice look like a Pop Warner player, Malik Shabazz Hayes.

"I guess the reason they asked me to give this speech was because Malik was my best friend. If they hadn't asked, I would have volunteered. Actually, besides my wife, he was my only friend.

"I suppose that when a good and talented guy dies young and senselessly, it's customary to rail against the injustice that took him away and, yes, it was injustice that took him away: racism from black people and from white people. It's God's grace that we haven't murdered each other off."

He looked at Felice again. She smiled sadly at him and nodded her head encouragingly. *You can get through this, Honey.*

"And I will talk about those depressing things in a minute, but right now, I want to talk about football." He flashed a grin at the crowd. "Some of you might remember the game we played against UCLA in December of 1991. In the last minute-thirty, the game was tied. We were on offense at their thirty. It was third and eight and Coach had given me the signal for a screen to the sideline near their twenty.

"We were in huddle and Malik says to me," Kevin's voice dropped an octave. "'Bomb me right in the zone, Lightnin.' That dumb-ass Jackson is droppin' off me.'"

Felice laughed along with the crowd at Kevin's near perfect imitation of Malik's Detroit street-kid accent.

"I said, 'Coach'll cut me if it doesn't work.' He said, 'It'll work. Do it.'

"So, I get under center and make the call. The ball's snapped." Kevin walked to the right of the lectern, his slight limp evident, and turned to his left, with the microphone in his right hand.

"I drop back and take a look. There's Malik, sure enough, headed toward right side of the end zone with that dumb-ass Jackson beaten. UCLA's coaches must have been dumb too because they had Malik in single coverage. I haul it." Kevin was going to mime passing the microphone to the end of the platform. As he looked long, past the end of the platform, he could see one of the goals on the practice field. He lowered the microphone. On the right side of the end zone, he thought he saw a tall, rangy figure suited-up in black, white and orange, his helmet gleaming in the sunshine. The figure was waving a gloved hand at him to make the toss. He thought he could make out the number on the jersey: eighty eight.

Kevin dropped the microphone. To his left, on his chair, there just happened to be a football. He picked it up and passed it with all his might in the direction of the figure in the end zone. He still had it! The ball reached its mark and Kevin thought he saw the figure catch the ball and start to do an end zone dance. Then the figure pointed in Kevin's direction, as if to say, "YOU!!"

At that moment, a light, cool, and unseasonable breeze blew through Kevin's long, graying hair--evaporating the sweat on his brow. It was a kind and comforting relief.

"Touchdown," Kevin laughed almost to himself. Then he remembered what he was there for. He turned to the crowd. For a moment, he had forgotten they existed. The only sound Kevin could hear was crying. Nearly everyone in the audience was in tears.

"Kevin..." Kevin whirled to his right. Felice had lumbered up onto the platform and he hadn't even noticed. He looked down at the platform and picked up the microphone.

"Honey, will you sit down, please," he said into the microphone as he led her to his chair. "I know it would be kind of appropriate if our firstborn came out on a football field, but I'd just as soon not have that happen." The crowd laughed as he headed back to the lectern.

"Nag, nag, nag." Felice's voice had been picked up by the mike and the crowd erupted into an even more raucous and cathartic laughter.

"Sorry, folks. I was in another dimension for a moment." The crowd cheered.

Two weeks later, Kevin stood on the balcony outside of the obstetrics waiting room at NMU hospital. Mentally, he knew that this building was the same one in which he had recovered from his gunshot wound, and the same place in which he had nearly gone out of his mind with grief and anger. But spiritually, it was now another place altogether. The road between *that* day and this one had had more twists than he could have imagined way back then. Way back then? It had only been four years since the murder of his friend and the end of his football career, but it almost seemed as though that life had been part of a mirror universe. He had just taken the bar exam, something he never would have dreamed of doing in that other life. The only way he knew for sure that that other life had been his was that it had one thing in common with his present life: Felice.

That other NMU hospital had seemed like a tomb, but this one, was all about life, the life of his and Felice's child.

Only now, since the dedication of the NMU's Malik Hayes Practice Facility, was he able to think about Malik without being overwhelmed with emotion. He had no idea how he would have borne it had Felice left him. In the months following the shooting, he had thought she might. He had been so full of bitterness that he tried to push everyone away, especially the one person whom he loved most. He stood now, shaking his head and smiling at his own remembered stupidity.

Well, Malik, I'm a dad now. Hopefully, my boy hasn't inherited too many of my moron genes. Malik would have had something sarcastic, and no doubt, hilarious to say about that one. Kevin looked dead into the spectacular sun, which was setting over the West Mesa. *Could you keep an eye on our boy when I'm not around, make sure he's okay?*

You know it, Lightnin'! said a voice inside Kevin's head. He turned, heading back in to kiss his wife and to marvel at his son.

Her mother hadn't been exaggerating when she had told her daughter how painful childbirth was. Felice had screamed and, yes, railed at her husband (who was in the delivery room), as the waves of each contraction had gripped her. But, finally, the doctor had pulled out that bawling, wriggling mass of human being that she and Kevin had created. A *huge* wriggling mass: ten pounds even and twenty-three inches long! She supposed that she had expected it to be so. She had weighed nine pounds herself at birth and Kevin, who had been a month premature, had, nevertheless, weighed a respectable six pounds, two ounces.

They had planned the arrival of their son perfectly, right after Kevin's graduation from NMU Law School. Felice herself was still in law school, but they hadn't wanted to wait any longer to start a family, especially not with her parents and Herbert Hart bugging them about it constantly.

The hospital room door opened, as the nurse brought her son in for feeding. Her son! *How can I be somebody's Mom? What if I forget to feed him or change him? What if I let something happen to him? What if someone does something to him? What in the hell were we thinking?* But there was no backing out now. The nurse was putting the child into her arms.

"Now, just remember what we told you dear," the middle-aged woman said. "It's not easy at first. Your milk may not come right away, so you might have to give him the bottle at first. I'll set it here."

"Okay. Thank you."

"Oh, it's my pleasure. That's a big, handsome boy you've got there. I like bringing him to you just so I can pick him up." The nurse smoothed the child's amazing mass of curly, dark hair.

"Well, let's see if I can do this." She untied the back of the hospital gown and pulled the front down just far enough to expose her right breast. She put her son's mouth next to the nipple. He immediately responded.

"I think there's some milk in there," Felice said as she looked hopefully at the nurse.

"Looks like it, hon." The boy was drinking enthusiastically. "Whadaya know? First try successful. Doesn't happen very often. Guess yours believes in eating."

"Just like his mother." Felice and the nurse looked up as Kevin walked through the door.

"I'll leave the new family alone now," the nurse said as she walked toward the door.

"Thanks," Felice called to her. "You're a pretty good nurse."

The woman, radiant, turned back to her. "Why thank you, sweetheart. And don't worry. You're already a wonderful mother."

Felice looked up at her.

"You first-timers are always scared," the nurse continued. "I was. Don't worry. It gets easier. I should know with my five."

"Whew!" Felice shook her head unable to grasp the thought of giving birth to that many children. "You're a better woman than I am."

"Maybe, maybe not. We'll see, won't we?" The nurse smiled and left them alone.

"Five, huh? Wanna get started tomorrow?" Kevin was sitting on the edge of the bed. With her right leg, Felice nearly caused him to fall on the floor.

"You'll be lucky if you get me to agree to number two. Let's just concentrate on big man here, shall we?"

"Gladly." Kevin stroked his son's hair.

A day later, there was a small, slightly rowdy crowd outside the maternity ward; all there to view the Hart baby. Felice's parents and brother, Kevin's father, Laura and Adrienne Anderson, and Amanda Bain were alternately knocking on the window and cooing at the new life. Joseph and Herbert were good-naturedly teasing each other about which grandfather the boy would be named for, while Vetra and Laura were trading war stories about their own experiences with childbirth. However, Amanda, Adrienne, and Joey were silently staring with wonder at the baby. The two young women were also eavesdropping on the reminiscences of the older women with a mixture of dread and anticipation. And Joey felt a decidedly strange, but not unpleasant sensation--mulling on the fact that he was an uncle.

Just then one of the nurses wheeled out Felice with Kevin walking beside the chair.

"Hi family!" exclaimed Felice. "Wanna see the kid up close and personal-like?" All shouted their assent.

The nurse went into the nursery, scooped up the child and brought him out. To the oohs and ahhs of the group, she slowly deposited him into Felice's arms.

Joseph was there first. He bent down on one knee. Misty-eyed, he kissed his first grandchild lovingly on the forehead.

"Welcome, Grandson. Your grandma and I welcome you into the world." He stood up. "Herb?"

Herbert smiled at Joseph and bent down to offer a benediction of his own. "I welcome you into the world, grandson. Your grandma Carla has gone to be with the Lord, but, hopefully, one day, a very, very long time from now, you'll get to meet her."

"Amanda." Felice turned her face towards her former nemesis, now trusted friend. "Come say 'hi' to Malik." Mandy's eyes widened, and then she smiled radiantly and walked over. But before she made her acquaintance with the baby, she kissed Felice on the forehead.

"Thank you."

One month later...

The church was packed with family and friends. Felice stood next to Kevin as they both watched their dozing son. The boy's head was nestled against Joey's shoulder. The older boy was now nearly fourteen, over six-feet, and still growing. The priest was explaining the duties of Godparents to him and to a majestic-looking Adrienne.

The infant fussed a bit as he shifted against his uncle's shoulder. Felice smiled as she watched Joey soothe her son.

"He's good with him," Kevin whispered to her.

"What a surprise that is," she whispered back. "Who'd have thought that a teenaged boy only interested in basketball, football, girls, and food would make the perfect baby-sitter?"

Kevin laughed and then cut it off as he spotted his mother-in-law's frown out of the corner of his eye.

Vetra's scowl briefly turned to a smile as she turned to look at Herbert Hart, who was standing next to her. He was clasping tightly the hand of his new wife, Laura Anderson.

The priest was speaking more loudly and every one in the church was immediately silent.

"I christen you Malik Shabazz Hart, in the Name of the Father, Son, and the Holy Spirit. May you always walk in the Spirit of the Lord and always call on the Name of Jesus Christ. Joseph LeCroix, Junior and Adrienne Anderson, you are charged with the spiritual upbringing of this child of the Lord. Do you accept your responsibilities?"

"We do," they said in unison.

"Then, I pronounce you the Godparents of this child of the Lord." He traced the sign of the cross on the boy's forehead.

"In the Name of the Father, Son, and the Holy Spirit." The entire church genuflected.

Just then, Malik looked up from Joey's shoulder. He seemed to be looking at his parents. A wide smile spread across his caramel-colored face.

Felice and Kevin looked at him, then smiled happily back at him.

Kevin put his arms around Felice.

"Malik's still with us," he whispered in wonder.

"Yes, my love. He still lives."